"13"

😊 LUV
NANNA

Stone Horse

PRAISE FOR THE MUSTANG MOUNTAIN SERIES

I read the "About the Author" part. You were just like me! I have imaginary horses like you did. I go to riding school, and in the summer I went to horse camp for one week. Please email me back!!
—Sincerely, Chloe

I love reading your books. They're filled with mystery, excitement, horses and everything I love in a book. I can spend hours reading them. I have just started #9 *Dark Horse* ... Wow, it's awesome! I can't wait till Mustang Mountain #10!! Hope you keep on writing!
—Horse-crazy Stevie

Did you ever get a feeling that you're best friends with some of the characters in the book? When I'm done reading the books, I'll miss Becky and Alison and Meg so much. So please write more books about Mustang Mountain Ranch!
—Cassie Hergott

These are the best books I've ever read. I just luv them. I'm 11 years old, but I can *so* connect with all of the girls in the books—it's like we're the same people. Anyway, are you going to write any more in the Mustang Mountain series?
—Jessica

Reading these books takes me into a whole new world, with excitement and adventure around every corner. I've never been to the Rocky Mountains, but I feel like I'm there every time I read your books. Since Meg, Alison and Becky are my age, it feels like I'm there with them. Please continue to write these books and take the three friends on many more adventures.
—Tabitha Carter

Sharon writes back to all the fans who write to her at her email address: sharon@sharonsiamon.com. Join the crowd!

10

MUSTANG MOUNTAIN

Stone Horse

Sharon Siamon

WALRUS
B O O K S

Edited by Lori Burwash
Proofread by Elizabeth McLean
Cover photos by Michael Burch and Mark Macdonald
Cover design by Roberta Batchelor
Interior design by Margaret Lee / Bamboo & Silk Design Inc.
Typesetting and cover layout by Five Seventeen / PicaPica.ca

Printed and bound in Canada.

Library and Archives Canada Cataloguing in Publication
Siamon, Sharon
    Stone horse / Sharon Siamon.

(Mustang Mountain; 10)
ISBN 1-55285-798-0
ISBN 978-1-55285-798-4

    1. Horses—Juvenile fiction. I. Title. II. Series: Siamon,
    Sharon Mustang Mountain ; 10.

PS8587.I225S76 2006   jC813'.54   C2006-900699-7

The publisher acknowledges the support of the Canada Council and
the Cultural Services Branch of the Government of British Columbia in
making this publication possible. Whitecap Books also acknowledges
the financial support of the Government of Canada through the Book
Publishing Industry Development Program for our publishing activities.

Please note: Some places mentioned in this book are fictitious
while others are not.

ANCIENT FOREST
FRIENDLY

The inside pages of this book are 100% recycled, processed chlorine-free
paper with 40% post-consumer content. For more information, visit
Markets Initiative's website: www.oldgrowthfree.com.

To David and Lynn Bennett

CONTENTS

Acknowledgments

I'd like to thank:

Lori Burwash, my terrific editor on the Mustang Mountain series for her knowledge, expertise, and helpful guidance.

Dr. Wayne Burwash, an equine practioner from the Calgary area, for helping me with the horse facts.

Duane Papke for taking me to see Alberta's wild horses and for sharing his knowledge of these amazing animals.

CHAPTER 1

Return to the Ranch

Meg O'Donnell tingled with excitement as the jet roared down the runway. She couldn't wait to soar above the smoggy city air. At the other end of this flight was everything she loved: the Rocky Mountains, Mustang Mountain Ranch and Thomas Horne.

When they'd said goodbye last July, Meg hadn't known when she'd see tall, dark-haired Thomas again. But now, here she was at the start of another summer's adventure. She'd be working with Thomas and her best friends Alison Chant and Becky Sandersen. She'd missed them so much this past year! Now they'd all be together at the ranch for two fabulous months.

True, Thomas hadn't answered her emails or telephone messages lately. Meg thought he might be in the back country looking for wild horses—far from a computer or even a phone. But she hoped—no, she was sure—he'd turn up at the ranch. They'd all come to help save Mustang Mountain Ranch. They had to!

As the jet rose into the air, Meg remembered the email from Becky that had set this whole trip in motion. Becky's family ran a government ranch that trained horses for wilderness park patrol.

"Dear Meggie," Becky had written, "I have some bad news. The government wants to shut down the ranch. We've been trying to think of ways to save it and have come up with the idea of a riding camp. Interested in a summer job? Low pay, but room and board thrown in? Mom and Dad think you'd make a great camp cook, after your experience last summer at Sunrise Lodge. Alison, Rob, Chuck and I have all agreed to be counselors. We thought Thomas might agree to work as a guide on outtrips. What do you think?"

What did she think? It would be fantastic! A horse camp for kids at Mustang Mountain Ranch? With all of them running it? Perfect. Meg wriggled impatiently in her seat. Too bad she'd missed the first week of camp because she had to babysit her little brother, but at last she was on her way. She'd be camp cook!

That last thought made Meg dive for her notebook tucked in the seat pocket. She'd copied recipes from her mom's cookbooks in her small, neat handwriting. She'd better study them before the plane landed in Calgary. In a few hours, she'd be cooking dinner for twenty-eight people!

At a small corral at the end of a dirt track, a ranch hand was waiting for Meg with Rascal, an Appaloosa mare. There were no roads to Mustang Mountain Ranch—she would have to ride for two hours on a wilderness trail. As she climbed into Rascal's saddle, Meg breathed in the fresh mountain air with delight. She was back where she belonged.

All the way up the twisting trail, Meg planned meals for the camp. Tonight they'd have barbecued steak with roast potatoes and a huge salad. Chocolate cake for dessert.

But seconds after arriving at the ranch, Meg realized she wouldn't need her recipes.

Alison was waiting for her at the gate. "I'm so, so glad you're here!" Alison grabbed for her hand. "I thought you'd never come."

Meg heard a catch in Alison's voice that was almost a sob. Her friend's shirt was untucked, her jeans baggy. Her smooth cap of dark hair almost stood on end. Meg had always seen Alison poised, perfectly groomed, with not a hair out of place. What was wrong?

Surprised, Meg dismounted and handed her horse's reins to the ranch hand. She threw her arms around Alison. "I'm sorry I couldn't be here to cook for the start of camp," Meg began to apologize, "but I'll make it up—"

"You won't be doing any cooking," Alison said as

they hurried across the yard to the house. "You're a camp counselor now—taking over from Rob Kelly. He came down with a bad virus and had to go home."

"Poor Rob. Poor Becky!" Meg set her heavy backpack on the ranch house porch with a thump. Rob was Becky's boyfriend. Meg could imagine how disappointed she must be not to have him here.

"I thought it would be so perfect," Alison rushed on. "The three of us and our three boyfriends—working at the camp for the whole summer. But now Rob's gone home and Chuck is boring me to death and we're so shorthanded. We need Thomas! When do you think he'll get here?"

Meg shook her head. "I don't know. I still haven't heard from him." Mustang Mountain Ranch looked just the same as ever—so beautiful it brought tears to her eyes. The ranch was set on the side of a high mountain meadow with towering peaks all around. It was the one place on Earth that Meg felt really and truly happy. It was so good to be back here that even without Thomas it was hard to feel anything except joy.

"... so for now it's just the four of us," Alison was saying. "Stuck with twenty wild kids and a lot of horses." Her dark eyes widened. "You look even more gorgeous than last summer, Meg. You're taller, and your eyes are such an amazing shade of blue."

Meg tugged on her long brown ponytail. She knew Alison was jealous of the way she looked. When they first came to Mustang Mountain three years ago, she'd been plain, dumpy Meg—Alison's invisible friend. Now she got lots of attention from guys of all ages. Not that it mattered. It was Thomas she cared about—and only Thomas!

Meg hurried to get off the subject of her looks. "Where are the kids?" she asked. "I didn't see any as I rode in."

"Becky has them out looking for fossils in the creek bed," Alison said. "All the rain last week washed away the banks, so you can find cool rocks."

"I heard about your floods, back east," said Meg. "Any damage?"

"Not really," Alison said. "Most of the flooding was lower down on the Red Deer and Panther rivers. But a week of rain has almost wrecked the camp. It's hard to have fun when it's pouring! We hope the out-trips will turn things around—your group leaves tomorrow."

"Tomorrow?" Meg gasped.

"Yep!" Alison nodded. "The kids are pretty pumped." She glanced at her watch. "They should be back in a few minutes—in Cabin 3. That's Slim's old bunkhouse, behind the main lodge." She hoisted Meg's bag on her shoulder. "You'd better go introduce yourself. I'll take your stuff up to our room. Thank heavens we don't have to sleep with the campers!"

This was so typical of Mustang Mountain, Meg thought as she sped to the bunkhouse. Plans changed suddenly. She'd no sooner got here than she was being sent off on a three-day trip with kids she didn't even know. But whatever happened, they had to make this camp a success. The ranch couldn't disappear—it just couldn't!

CHAPTER 2

MEET THE CAMPERS

Ten minutes later, Meg's campers straggled into the bunkhouse—four girls, aged eleven and twelve, all shapes and sizes.

"*Camp Loser*, that's what they should call this place!" A short girl with wild frizzy hair plopped on a bunk and glared at Meg.

"Why? Wh-what do you mean?" Meg stammered.

"It rained for four solid days when we got here. Now Bossy Becky has us sloshing through a muddy creek looking for rocks. I feel like I've got moss growing between my toes!" The girl stuck out a soggy boot for Meg to inspect.

"Yeah, and our counselor got sick and left. We're in the worst cabin in this loser camp," a tall girl with straight black bangs and glasses shot in. "Look at this dump!"

Meg had looked. When she walked into the small bunkhouse, she'd been shocked. The floor was covered in dirty socks and underwear, beds were unmade, and empty drawers hung open. The bathroom was even worse—wet smelly towels and clothes heaped everywhere.

"Why don't you clean it up?" Meg asked. "It doesn't have to be a dump."

"What's the use?" The frizzy-haired girl shrugged. "It'll just get messy again, and nothing ever dries out."

"Rob never made us clean up," the tall girl in glasses added. She stood with her hands on her hips, staring Meg down.

"But if we're going on this out-trip tomorrow, you'll have to organize your stuff and get packed," Meg pointed out. "C'mon, I'll give you a hand."

Four hostile faces stared at her. No one moved.

"All right," sighed Meg. "Let's start again. I'm Meg O'Donnell, your new counselor. I'm sixteen, and I've been coming to Mustang Mountain Ranch since I was thirteen. Now, let's hear your names and how old you are."

The silence was total.

"Fine." Meg turned with a shrug. Her brother had more attitude in his skinny little finger than all four of these girls put together! "Suit yourselves," she said. "I'll get your names from the camp register in the office." She headed out the bunkhouse door. "See you later."

"Wait!" The frizzy-haired girl jumped to her feet. "All right ..." She turned to the others. "We may as well tell her our names, if she's going to be our counselor. I'm Rachel, I'm twelve. And this is Courtney." She pointed to the girl in glasses. "We call her Daddy Longlegs because she's so tall."

"Shut up!" Courtney stuck out her tongue at Rachel. "I'm the oldest one here—I'll be thirteen in a few weeks."

"And this lovely creature is Cam." With a flourish, Rachel pointed to a blonde, green-eyed girl on the bunk beside her. "She's rich, and her father is some government big shot."

Cam's smooth forehead creased in a frown. "You don't have to say things like that. Who my father is has nothing to do with me."

"Whatever." Rachel shrugged. "*Anyway* ... That's Dee-Dee, the one with the teddy bear."

A tiny brown-haired girl on the bed nearest Meg hugged a bedraggled bear to her chest. "My real name is Deanna," she said, "but they call me Dee-Dee." She giggled. "I'm eleven, I'm gifted, and I talk too much."

"That's only four of you. There are supposed to be five ..." Meg began. "Where is ..." Just then the door burst open behind her.

"Why didn't you guys wait for me?" A slight, fair-haired girl with large hazel eyes stumbled across the doorstep, spilling rocks from her overloaded arms. "I couldn't walk fast with all these stones."

She started taking rocks out of every pocket, the hood of her sweatshirt and even the inside of her baseball cap. They clattered to the floor, adding mud to the dirt already there.

Rachel sighed. "And this is Jordan. She just turned eleven—"

"She's *always* late!" Dee-Dee broke in.

"We always have to wait for her," Courtney complained. "We come in last in every competition. No wonder we're the loser cabin." She pulled her glasses down and glared at Jordan over their tops. "Did you have to bring every rock in the river?"

Jordan looked at the floor. "Sorry!" she apologized again. "I'll clean it up."

Meg felt an instant sympathy for Jordan. Before she met Alison and Becky, she'd been a shy, awkward girl herself. She kept her face neutral. If she let the other campers know how sorry she felt for Jordan, they'd be even harder on her.

"Thanks for the introductions," she told Rachel. "I'll go check in with the other counselors now."

"They'll be in the ranch house, having a *fabulous* time," Rachel sighed. "You counselors have all the fun around here. We're just the lowly slaves."

Meg ignored that. "See what you can do to get this bunkhouse in shape and I'll come and help you pack later," she said firmly.

At that moment a loud bell clanged in the yard outside.

The four campers shot to their feet. "Can't clean it now!" Courtney shouted as she dashed past Meg in the doorway. "That's the bell for our riding lesson."

She and the others streaked across the ranch yard, heading for the barn and corrals like a bunch of young horses, with Jordan bringing up the rear.

"Nice to meet you, Rachel, Courtney, Cam, Dee-Dee and Jordan," Meg murmured after their disappearing backs. She picked up a few damp towels from the floor and tossed them into an overflowing laundry basket. Mustang Mountain Ranch Camp was not turning out the way she had pictured it.

CHAPTER 3
RIDING LESSON

When Meg reached the barn, her five campers and another five from a different cabin were already starting to saddle their horses.

Becky stood in the middle of the group. She was Alison's first cousin, but the two girls looked totally different. While Alison was dark-haired, Becky had fair curly hair and hazel eyes. She gave Meg a quick welcoming wave and went on with her lesson. Meg was dying to rush over and throw her arms around her friend, but Becky was too busy for hugs. The Cabin 3 campers were giving her a tough time.

"Are we just going to ride around the corral in stupid circles, *again*?" Courtney complained, hauling on her horse's cinch.

"When do we get to do some *real* riding?" sighed Dee-Dee. "This is so bor-ring!"

"Tomorrow," Becky told her. "And once you're on the trail, you'll be glad you've put in so many practice hours."

Becky saw Cam, who was slipping the bridle on her horse with practiced ease, give a doubtful shrug. Cam's lovely face stayed calm, but it was clear what she was thinking. All this was a waste of her time.

"Whew!" Meg whistled under her breath. What would three days on the trail with this bunch be like?

"Come on, Jordan!" Rachel's voice broke into Meg's thoughts. "You're holding us up again!"

Meg turned to see Jordan struggling with her saddle. She had barely started to tack up the dapple gray, while the other girls were already either mounted or had finished doing up their bridles. Jordan's horse was snorting and tossing his head, showing total disrespect for his rider.

"Meg!" Becky called. "Can you give her a hand with Rocco?"

"Sure!" Meg reached for Rocco's bridle and saw Becky's grateful grin brighten her face.

Rachel and Courtney were rolling their eyes at Jordan, which only made her more flustered and fumbly.

"Don't pay any attention to them," Meg whispered. "You're doing fine."

"Can you finish tacking up for me?" begged Jordan. "I can never remember what goes where."

"I will, this time," Meg promised. "But after this, you'll have to do it yourself."

She handed the bridle to Jordan. "Hold it like you would a handlebar on a bike," she told her. "Don't fold his ears back, fold them forward under the headpiece. That's better—a horse with his ears back is an angry horse, no matter how his ears got that way. And hold your left hand flat. That's right, make sure the bit's right in his mouth. Don't worry, horses have no teeth back there."

"C'mon! We're tired of waiting for her," roared Rachel. "She should know how to do it by now."

"I know I should," mumbled Jordan, flushing. "But the more I hurry, the slower it goes."

Meg sped through the rest of the tacking up with practiced skill and boosted Jordan up on Rocco's back. The gray horse did a little crow hop, just to register his disapproval, and then settled down as Jordan rode him over to the group.

That horse needs to learn some respect, thought Meg. If Thomas was here to train him ... She sighed. Of course she had come here to help make the camp a success and save Mustang Mountain, but everything here reminded her of Thomas. If only she could turn around, right now, and see him riding across the yard on his beautiful Appaloosa, Palouse. Would he ever get here?

🐛

The lesson over, Meg walked with Becky back to the house.

"This is our sanctuary!" Becky closed the office door. She brushed back her blonde curls, and her usually rosy face creased in a frown. "The campers are never allowed in here—it's the only place we can get away from them."

"The girls in my cabin think you escape here to have wild parties." Meg laughed.

Becky collapsed in her father's baggy old leather chair. "Do they?" She chuckled weakly. "If those kids could only see us after a day spent dragging them around this ranch. We all collapse like punctured balloons. And it's still not over—we have campfire every night!"

She groaned. "I'm so glad you're here. Since Rob had to leave, it's been a nightmare." Becky looked up at Meg with weary brown eyes. "Mom used to run a riding camp before she got married, so she thought she could do it here, but ..." She paused and shook her head. "Nothing's working out the way we thought!"

"I'm sorry I couldn't get here for the start of camp," Meg apologized. "How is Rob?"

Becky frowned again. "I wish I knew ... he was really sick. They say it's a virus, but I'm so worried it's something worse."

Just then, Alison and her boyfriend, Chuck, burst through the door. "Fifteen minutes to catch our breath before the dinner gong!" Alison panted.

Chuck McClintock was large and sturdy, with thick red hair and a wide grin. "Great to see you, Meg," he puffed. "Now if Thomas would just show up. Any idea where he is?"

Meg shook her head.

"He's supposed to be guiding the out-trip tomorrow,"

Becky added. "Dad's trying frantically to get a substitute, but it's hard."

"Maybe the idea of going off in the wilderness with five giddy girls made Thomas run for the hills." Chuck grinned. He and Thomas had been friends for a long time.

"You might be right," Meg confessed. "But he might just be somewhere in the back country and didn't get our messages. Couldn't we put off the out-trip for a few days and see if he arrives?"

"That's impossible," Becky moaned from the depths of her chair. "The kids have been looking forward to this trip since they got here."

"It's all they talk about," Alison agreed. She flopped on a leather loveseat and Chuck squeezed in close beside her. "Your group goes first. Then we need time for each of the other three groups to go before the end of this session, with time for the horses to rest in between. We can't put it off, or one of the groups won't get their trip."

"We planned everything so carefully," Becky sighed. "But we didn't count on all that rain and Rob getting sick and you being late and Thomas not showing up at all!"

"So who will go with me?" Meg looked anxiously around her small group of friends.

"I'm coming." Alison shrugged her slim shoulders. "Even though the kids in your cabin hate me. They call me Alley Cat for some reason."

Meg hid a grin. The campers were deadly accurate with their nicknames. Alison *did* look like a sleek cat. And she could be as cool and aloof as a cat at times.

"Here comes Dad." Becky peered out the window. "Maybe he's got some news about another wrangler for the out-trip."

CHAPTER 4

JESSE

Becky's father, Dan Sandersen, strode into the office wearing a smile as wide as the prairie sky. "It's all fixed," he crowed. "Jesse Martin just rode in. He's ready to leave first thing tomorrow to lead your out-trip."

Crossing the office in one long step, Dan reached for Meg's hand. "Welcome, Meg. Thanks for helping us out."

"My pleasure!" Meg said.

Behind her, she could hear Alison gasp. "Jesse—not *the* Jesse? The one from our first summer here?"

"The same cowboy. Didn't you rescue him from a grizzly bear or something?" Dan teased.

Alison's face turned pink. "We—uh—saved each other," she stammered. "I haven't seen him for three years!"

"You never told me about this guy, Jesse." Chuck studied Alison's flushed face in surprise.

"Oh—didn't I?" Alison stood up suddenly. "Well, we'd better go and say hello. C'mon, Meg, Becky!" Alison grabbed them both by the hand and headed for the door, leaving Chuck sitting on the loveseat, his mouth open.

As they crossed the ranch yard, Alison draped her arms around Becky's and Meg's shoulders. "It'll be so weird seeing Jesse again," she said breathlessly. "He probably won't even remember me."

"Of course he will," Becky scoffed. "You don't beat off a grizzly bear attack with someone and forget them."

"I was so crazy about him ... remember?"

"How could we forget?" Memories came rushing back to Meg—Alison scheming and plotting to get Jesse's attention that first summer at the ranch. It didn't matter that Jesse was too old for her. At thirteen, Alison had an enormous crush on the young ranch hand.

Becky gave her cousin a mischievous glance. "I wonder if Jesse married that pilot he was dating—Julie— was that her name?"

"That's right!" Alison's face fell. "I forgot about her."

"Anyway," Meg reminded Alison, "you've got Chuck now."

"Yeah," Alison sighed, "there's always Chuck."

"Don't you like him?" asked Meg. "I thought you two had been dating since last October."

"Of course I *like* Chuck." Alison dropped her arms from her friends' shoulders. "If only he didn't pant at my feet like a big fuzzy dog all the time."

"Alison!" Becky burst into giggles. "What a thing to say!"

"He's better than a guy who's always off chasing wild horses," said Meg. "Thomas promised he'd be here when I came back, but for him, *here* is the whole wilderness. He could be anywhere from here to Rocky Mountain House!"

"If you ask me, it's romantic. You never know when Thomas will ride in on Palouse ..." Becky sighed.

Alison jolted to a halt, staring at the corral. "There's Jesse! What should I do?"

Jesse was leaning against the fence watching his black horse, Tailor, with his boot on the bottom fence rail and his hat tipped over his eyes.

"Should I go over and talk to him?" Alison gasped.

"Seems like you're not the only one with that idea." Becky grinned. "Look!" Before they could cross the yard, the five girls from Cabin 3 had surrounded Jesse. It was as if their boy radar had flashed "cool-looking cowboy at the corral." Only Cam and Jordan hung back a little, and even they looked impressed.

"They're like wasps on a hamburger," cried Alison. "Poor Jesse!" He had shoved his hat farther down his forehead and hunched his shoulders.

"Girls!" Becky called. "Aren't you supposed to be getting washed up for dinner?"

"We're just saying hello, if you don't mind," Rachel wheeled around to tell her. "He *is* going to be the wrangler on our out-trip, isn't he?"

"Yes, if you don't scare him away." Becky marched forward. "Cabin 3, this is Jesse Martin. Jesse, meet the campers you're taking on the trail for three days. This is Courtney, Rachel, Cam, Dee-Dee and Jordan."

Jesse's grin lit up his sun-weathered face. He pushed back his hat. "Glad to meet you all," he drawled. "Now excuse me while I say hello to some old friends." He strode through the group of girls, spreading his arms wide.

"It's good to see you, Meg, Becky." Jesse's smile brightened. "And you!" He stared at Alison. "You've grown up some, Al. Lookin' good."

Alison felt her heart melt. Jesse was the only person who'd ever called her Al. Three years ago, he'd shown her she wasn't just a spoiled city kid—that she could be brave and risk her life for somebody else. She'd even smacked a grizzly bear with a rock to save Jesse ... her head spun with memories, old feelings surged to the surface.

"You—look fine, too," she heard herself stammer.

The five campers gaped at the two of them.

"She knows him," Courtney muttered to the other campers. "Did you see how she looked at him?"

"C'mon, gang." Meg herded the five campers toward their bunkhouse, leaving Becky and Alison with Jesse. "Show me the routine you follow before dinner."

"There is no *routine*," Rachel said gloomily. "We're supposed to get washed and presentable for the dining room, but who cares?"

"Have you seen our bathroom?" Dee-Dee shrilled. "It's disgusting. I'll bet there are mushrooms growing in the shower."

"Well, if there are, it's your fault!" Meg blasted them. "You have to shape up if you're going on a three-day trail ride with Jesse," she went on. "He won't stand for any sloppiness. When Alison and I first met Jesse, we were fresh from the city. Neither of us had ever ridden in the mountains, or even ridden western. He taught us a thing or two ..."

"Tell us!" Rachel demanded. "Tell us everything Jesse did, everything he said."

For the first time since I got here, Meg thought, they're really listening to me. This is good. She looked at the five eager faces. I wonder how long I can string out this story.

The girls were obviously in awe of Jesse, and who wouldn't be? The shy nineteen-year-old had morphed into a champion rodeo cowboy. From his silver buckle to his weathered face, he's earned that look of a champion, Meg thought, and he's here helping the Sandersens as a favor because Mustang Mountain is a special place for him, too. If only they could make this out-trip a success.

CHAPTER 5

A Spy in the Camp?

Leaving the campers to get ready for dinner, Meg hurried to the main barn. There was one person at Mustang Mountain she still hadn't seen.

She hoped to find Laurie Sandersen, Becky's mom, working in the barn. For three summers, Laurie had been almost like her own mom. Laurie understood about Thomas, and Meg could sure use some of that understanding now.

Sure enough, Laurie was bent over a horse's hoof in the center aisle. She was a slight, wiry woman, and as she glanced up from her task, Meg could see new lines in her face, creased by worry and hard work over the past year.

"Meg!" She straightened slowly. "I'm sorry I wasn't

here to say hi when you arrived, but I was out on the trail with a horse."

Meg said quickly, "It's me who's sorry. I wanted to get here for the beginning of camp, but I had to babysit my brother."

"That's okay. Slim's filling in as camp cook." Laurie patted the tall bay in the crossties. "I thought you might like to ride Cody here."

"Thanks. You remembered how much I love Cody!" Meg exclaimed. She went over to rub the gentle gelding's long brown nose. "How are you, big fella? Next to my own horse, Patch, you're the best horse in the world."

"He needs a new shoe, but otherwise he's in good shape." Laurie stroked Cody's glossy hide. "I hope he and the other horses are up for a three-day trip." She sighed. "I thought a riding camp would be such a good idea. I thought we'd start small and grow. But even with only twenty campers, we're struggling."

"I'm sure the trip will be great ... now that Jesse's here," said Meg. "The girls in my cabin seem excited."

"I hope you're right." Laurie led Cody back to his stall. "One of your campers is the heritage minister's daughter. It will be his decision whether to close the ranch or keep it open."

"Which camper?" Meg gasped.

"Cam. Camille Perrault."

"The quiet one with the blonde hair?"

Laurie nodded as she removed Cody's halter and handed it to Meg.

Meg fingered the worn halter. "You don't think Cam's father sent her here as a spy, do you?"

"I try not to think so." Laurie shut Cody's stall door. "She's one of the best riders we've got, so she's not faking an interest in horses. But if this out-trip is a disaster, we're in big trouble."

She smiled and changed the subject. "Tell me about Thomas. What do you suppose has happened to him?"

"I don't know," Meg sighed. "I was so excited to see him."

"This isn't the first time he's disappointed you, is it?"

"No," Meg admitted. "The truth is, if he sees that a wild stallion has left a stud pile on the trail, he's off chasing him without a look over his shoulder. I'll always come second to wild horses with Thomas."

"Not second, exactly." Laurie patted her arm. "He knows you'll wait, but the horses can't. There are only a few bands of wildies left in Alberta."

"That's the problem! He knows I'll hang around like an old saddle blanket—that I care about him more than anything!"

"I think he cares, too," Laurie said gently. "Some guys just don't know how to show it."

"Not good enough!" Meg protested. "He should be here. He's let *everyone* down, not just me. I'm going on the out-trip with Alison and Jesse and I'm not going to waste a single thought on him!"

"Glad to hear it." Laurie gave her a warm smile. "We're counting on you, Meg O'Donnell."

Just then, the dinner bell split the silence of the big old barn. The horses neighed in response.

"I guess we'd better go," Laurie said. "I'm the one who opens the dining room door and lets the starving campers in!"

"Another great Mustang Mountain Camp dinner! What will we be having? Minced moose on toast?" Dee-Dee pretended to throw up over the porch rail as Meg hurried to the house.

"Maybe fried squirrel?" Courtney suggested. "Or broiled beaver?"

"Who knows?" Rachel groaned.

Meg choked back her fury. How dare those girls complain about the food! Meg knew how hard it was to cook for a big group, and Slim wasn't even really a cook—just a retired cowboy.

Laurie had slipped around through the kitchen door to open the door to the dining room. She pointed to a table on the right as the campers stampeded past Meg. "That's Cabin 3's table."

"What's the big hurry if they hate the food?" Meg muttered to herself, heading for it.

She soon found out.

All five of Meg's campers were seated at their table holding their noses as she arrived.

"Is this some kind of protest?" she asked.

The girls were all pointing at her and choking with laughter.

"You're the gopher! You're the gopher!" they shrieked in unison. "Don't sit down. You've got to *go* to the kitchen *for* our food."

"What are you talking about?" Meg looked from one red face to another.

"We all do an action, like hands on our heads, stomping our feet or holding our noses. The last one to join in is the gopher. She has to go and get all our food from the kitchen," Rachel explained with satisfaction.

"—and clear away our dirty dishes, like a maid," Cam observed calmly.

Courtney stabbed her finger at Meg. "This time, you're it."

"All right. I get it." Meg threw up her arms. "It's a camp tradition. I'll play along this time—but you won't catch me again!"

"I'll help." Jordan pushed back her chair. "I'm usually the gopher anyway."

Meg saw the others roll their eyes.

"Never mind." Meg smiled at Jordan. "I know my way to the kitchen."

She wove through the tables to the swinging kitchen doors. Inside, a long table was spread with bowls of rice and meat, platters of bread and jugs of juice. Meg watched the other gophers stagger out the swinging doors carrying large trays. She wondered how skinny little Jordan managed a load like that.

As she filled her tray, she called out a greeting to Slim, who was bent over a big black pot. "Hi, Slim."

"Howdy, Meg. I see they got you workin', too." He waved a wooden spoon at her. "I can't keep up with what these kids eat!"

Back at Cabin 3's table, Courtney peered suspiciously at the meat in the bowl. "Squirrel stew—I was right!" she announced.

Rachel took a deep sniff. "Wrong. Curried squirrel on rice."

There were groans and gagging sounds around the table. Most of the kids pushed their plates away and grabbed for slices of bread.

Meg had had enough. "You don't deserve to get fed," she burst out. "I'm hauling this food right back to the kitchen!"

The five girls stopped making faces and stared at her. She could feel their hostility sweep over her. "When we're on the out-trip," she said steadily, "the first person who complains about the food has to cook for everybody else for the rest of the trip. *That's* the tradition on out-trips." She was making this up, but it worked. The hostile glares turned to unsure glances.

"Is that Jesse's rule?" Rachel asked at last.

"Of course," Meg said. "It's the rule of the trail. Everybody knows it."

"Where *is* Jesse?" Dee-Dee scrunched up her eyes, peering around the dining room.

"Getting stuff ready for the trip, which is what we have to do right after dinner," Meg said. She sat down and dug into the curry. It *was* awful! Slim was doing his best as a fill-in, but he must be cooking what he thought the kids would like instead of the plain ranch food he usually made. He'd probably never tasted curry in his life.

Dessert was worse—some kind of watery vanilla goop with slices of gray banana buried in it. When I get back from this out-trip, Meg promised herself, I'll have a talk with Slim!

After dinner, Laurie stood on the raised hearth of the massive stone fireplace and banged a spoon on a pot lid. "Attention, campers! I have an important announcement."

CHAPTER 6

NIGHT SECRETS

"Listen up!" Laurie had to shout over the din. "There will be no campfire tonight because the girls from Cabin 3 have to get ready to leave on their out-trip at six tomorrow morning."

There were groans of disappointment from around the tables.

"Campfire is my favorite part of this camp," mourned Dee-Dee.

"And tonight—" Laurie raised her voice and banged her pot lid for silence, "tonight I want to issue a challenge to Cabin 3. Since this is the first year of Mustang Mountain Ranch Camp and the first out-trip, you girls have a special responsibility—to bring back a trophy from your trip that will set a standard for all trips to come. It has to be somethin' you find on the trail, a bone, a piece of wood, a set of antlers. It should represent your courage, teamwork and wilderness skills. We'll display your trophy and future out-trip trophies on this mantle." She pointed to the deep shelf above the fireplace. "So good luck to Cabin 3 and get a good sleep."

There was silence in the room for a moment, then everyone started talking at once. Meg stood up and began to load the tray with dirty dishes to take back to the kitchen.

"Wait a minute," Cam said in a low voice. "I have an idea where to find a great trophy."

Meg stared at her in surprise. Cam's expressionless face looked almost excited. What had sparked this sudden interest?

"We're swearing you to secrecy!"

Later, in Cabin 3, five eager faces looked up at Meg from their bunks.

"No one can know where we're headed," Rachel insisted. "It *has* to be a secret."

"All right. I promise." It was lights-out time, and Meg was making a final check on Cabin 3.

"Tell her, Cam," Rachel went on. "Tell her your idea for the trophy."

Cam's green eyes glittered. "There's a legend," she said, "about Mustang Mountain. My dad came across it in one of his reports, and he told me about it. There's a cave in the stone horse at the top of the mountain."

"I've seen the stone horse." Meg nodded. Her sketchbook was full of drawings of it. Lit by the morning sun, it looked exactly like the head of a running mustang.

"The cave is in the horse's nostril," Cam rushed on, "and in it, there's supposed to be a deposit of pure jade—"

"If that's true," Meg interrupted, "wouldn't someone have found it by now?"

"Maybe not. Dad says there's lots of jade that's easier to mine. Or maybe it's not a big enough deposit to bother with. But it would be big enough for our trophy. We could ride up to it on this trip, if we had the nerve."

"It might be too difficult a climb for a three-day trip." Meg shook her head. "Jesse will know. We can ask him, but he's the guide and it's his decision."

"He has to let us!" Rachel threw back her covers and bounced out of her bed. "Everybody will be so knocked out when we come back with real jade. I can't wait!"

"Well, I'll ask him," Meg promised. "But we'd all better get to sleep if we're going to try to make it to the top of Mustang Mountain."

The idea of a quest for a trophy had changed the atmosphere in the cabin. All the girls were buzzing with excitement, but the biggest change was in Cam. She sat, hugging her knees, her face alive with the idea of finding a trophy in the stone horse.

Meg flipped off the light and stood in the dim

bunkhouse doorway until all the rustling and shifting stopped. "Think you can settle down?"

"We will," said Rachel firmly. "I'll sit on anyone who starts talking."

There were muffled giggles from the other bunks.

"All right. Good night." Meg went out and shut the door.

The sky to the west over the mountain peaks was still purple with the long July twilight. Soon the moon would rise and stars would blanket the sky over the ranch—millions of pinpricks of light—something Meg never saw in the city. She took a deep breath of the clear mountain air and wondered for the thousandth time that day where Thomas was.

"I'll leave a note for him with Chuck," she said out loud as she headed for the house. "That way, he'll know where we've gone and I won't exactly be breaking my promise not to tell the secret."

Meanwhile, Alison was packing in the room she shared with Meg. She knew that she should take the minimum of clothing—the less the horses had to carry, the better. Still, she'd have to take her new black shirt and at least two pairs of jeans ... and that purple fleece jacket that looked so good on her.

Alison rolled everything as tightly as she could and stuffed it hard into a small bag. There was a tap on the door and Chuck's broad face peered around its edge.

"Busy?" he asked.

"I'm packing." Alison felt a stab of annoyance. "It's late, and I have to get this done and get some sleep."

Chuck, as usual, didn't take the hint.

"I'm going to miss you," he sighed, coming in and planting himself in the room's only chair.

"It's only three days!" Alison stuffed more clothes in her pack, not looking at Chuck. "I'll be glad to get away from here."

"I know what you mean. It's been rough."

"Well, maybe Thomas will show up, and Rob will come back ..." Alison said lamely. She didn't believe either of those things would happen. "And now that Jesse's here ..."

"He seems like a nice fella." Chuck stood up. "What does he do in the rodeo?"

"I don't know." Alison shrugged, trying to keep her feelings off her face. "You'll have to ask him."

"I ride broncs and rope steers." Jesse appeared in the doorway, with Meg at his heels.

"And he's good at it," Meg added. "Two times national champion, isn't that right, Jesse?"

"I guess, but we didn't come up here to talk about rodeo," Jesse said. "Thought we'd better have a short meeting about this out-trip we're takin' tomorrow. Plan our route."

"I'll go then," Chuck said quickly. "See you tomorrow, Alison."

He disappeared out the door with a wistful glance at her.

He knows I like Jesse! Alison squirmed. Chuck had always been able to see right through her—it was no use trying to hide her feelings.

Jesse seemed to fill all the space in the small room. Alison's throat felt dry, and her knees started to shake. "Can—can we go downstairs to talk?" She cleared her throat. "There's not much space up here."

"Just what I was about to suggest," Jesse said in his low drawl. "I don't feel too comfortable in a girl's bedroom, even if it's just kids like you."

Kids? His words scorched Alison all the way down the stairs. Was that how he thought of her? Still the little kid he'd known three years ago? Well, she'd soon show him!

Sitting around a table in the dimly lit dining room, Alison and Jesse listened as Meg told them about Cam's idea for the trophy quest.

"Is it possible?" Alison asked Jesse. "Is there a safe route up to the stone horse?"

"Sure." Jesse nodded. "It's safe enough, but I can think of easier places to go for a three-day wilderness ride."

"Let's try to get there," Meg insisted. "The girls are so fired up about getting to the horse's head and bringing back something from the cave ... Cam looks like a different girl."

"And Cam isn't just another camper," Alison added. "She's the daughter of the cabinet minister who could shut down the ranch. If we make her happy, she'll give her dad a great report on the camp."

Meg nodded. "If we don't go ... it might mean the end of Mustang Mountain Ranch."

"I get it." Jesse chuckled. "Well, you girls haven't changed. Still itchin' to get into trouble any way you know how. Sure," he added, "we'll get up to that cave and look for jade in the stone horse's nose, if that's what it takes to save the ranch."

Alison burst out, "We have *so* changed—a lot."

Jesse got up and stretched. "I'm sure you have." He smiled down at her. "Still too early to turn in. How about a game of cards?"

"Okay," Alison said with a grin. "Just prepare to lose."

"I'm too tired," Meg yawned. "This morning, I was on the other side of the continent!" She left them and went out to look at the stars. "Oh, Thomas, where are you?" she asked the dome of twinkling lights. "Is Jesse right? Are we asking for trouble? I wish you were here to tell me."

CHAPTER 7

COLD START

"Are we going to the stone horse?"

Five sleepy faces greeted Meg and Alison the next morning as the campers emerged from the barn leading their horses.

At six, the air was chill. The horses' breath steamed from their nostrils, and the girls stood, shivering, as Jesse prepared a packhorse and Tailor to leave.

"Yes." Meg smiled at them. "We'll try to bring back a trophy from the horse's nose. If it's not jade, maybe we can find something else just as good."

"It'll be jade," Cam insisted. "I know it's there." Her blonde hair was pulled back in a tight knot at the base of her neck, but she looked as if she hadn't slept. There were dark circles shading the pale skin under her eyes.

"Let's go," she said impatiently, flinging her leg over her bay horse, Spencer.

The other campers were struggling to get mounted.

"My fingers are stiff from the cold. I can't get this stupid buckle undone." Courtney fumbled with a saddle-bag buckle.

"At least your horse stands still!" Rachel groaned. Her horse, Shane, was a black quarter horse/Canadian horse mix with short sturdy legs and a frizzy forelock that stuck out in a comical imitation of Rachel's own hair. He danced around, making it hard for Rachel to get her foot in the stirrup.

Dee-Dee was shivering from her toes to her bluish lips. "I—I hope y-you b-behave, Cl-cloudy," her teeth chattered as she clambered aboard the Appaloosa. "Why d-do they always g-give me the tallest horse when I'm the sh-shortest p-person?"

"Where's Jordan?" Alison glanced around the group.

"She's still in the barn, trying to get Rocco out of his stall," muttered Cam. "At this rate, we'll never make it out the gate, never mind to the stone horse."

"That's right." Alison looked sharply at the blonde girl. "So why don't you go and give her a hand, since you're ready?"

"If you say so." Cam dismounted, handed her reins to Alison and stomped off toward the barn.

"Cam's been like a drill sergeant since we woke up." Dee-Dee rolled her eyes. "*Come on! Hurry! Let's go!* That's all we heard."

"I think I liked her better when all she cared about was her hair," Courtney agreed.

"But she's right," sighed Rachel. "We'll never get the trophy if we don't get going."

There was stomping and whinnying from inside, then Cam appeared, leading Rocco at a fast clip. He was a powerfully built dapple gray. Jordan stumbled along behind, Rocco's heavy saddle in her arms, the stirrups trailing in the dirt.

Rocco stamped away from the saddle as Jordan tried to sling it over his back. "Stop that!" Cam ordered. "Stand still."

Rocco obeyed, but his clamped tail and pinned-back ears showed he didn't like it.

That overanxious tone in Cam's voice would never work, Meg thought.

"Here, let me," she said, taking the lead rope from Cam's clenched fist. Jordan would need every scrap of Rocco's strength and courage if they were to make it to the top, and it wasn't a good idea to start out with the horse mad at the world.

"It's all right," Meg murmured to Rocco, stroking his neck as Cam stepped aside. She could feel the gray horse relax as the threat of the blonde girl's anger was removed.

"You have to be firm with him, but not bossy," Meg explained to Jordan. "He has to trust you as his leader."

"I try." Jordan's hazel eyes were still scared and unsure. "I love horses *so* much, and I thought I'd love riding, but I'm no good! I can't make Rocco go where I want, or listen to me, or anything!"

Meg wished she could help Jordan stop feeling like the lowest rung of a ladder, but there wasn't time. Jesse was shouting directions.

"Put everything you want handy in your saddle-bags," he told them. "I don't want to see anything flopping around your neck, like a camera. When you're sure you're ready," he went on, "stand beside your horse in a line so I can check you out."

With Jesse giving orders, the girls sprang into action.

Fifteen minutes later, they were ready to go, even Jordan. The horses were lined up for inspection, the pink glow of the morning sun glimmering on their manes.

As Jesse started down the row, checking cinches and bridles, Becky came running from the house. "Mom and Dad said I should come with you!" she cried breathlessly. "They've called some friends. Ruby's coming from Sunrise Lodge to cook, and Claire, the park warden, has a few days off, so she's riding over."

"That's great news!" Meg beamed. "Who's going to look after your campers while you're gone?"

"Mom volunteered. She said this out-trip has to be a success and I've got more long-distance riding experience than anyone." This was true. Becky had competed in a fifty-mile endurance race the autumn before. "It'll just take me a minute to saddle Shadow," she gasped. She dashed off in the direction of the barn to get her brown and white paint.

"Another holdup," grumbled Cam. "Are we *ever* going to leave?"

"You'll be glad Becky came along," Meg said, giving Cody's saddle blanket a twitch. "She knows these mountains better than anyone except Jesse."

"It will be just like old times, the three of us setting out on a horse trek." Alison gave her horse, Lucky, a loving pat. "With Jesse leading us up the mountain."

"Remember how you made fun of him?" Meg teased. "You called him a hick cowboy, as I remember."

"I was an idiot," Alison laughed. "A complete idiot!"

Alison never did anything halfway, Meg thought. If she was crazy about Jesse, it was the passion of a lifetime—even though Alison's passions never lasted longer than an ice cream cone on a hot day.

Right now, Jesse was walking toward Alison, and Meg could almost see her friend's knees wobble.

"This is a nice-lookin' horse, Al." Jesse ran his knowledgable fingers over her bay's dark flank. Lucky had black socks and a white patch on his forehead in the shape of a four-leaf clover. "Where'd you find him?"

Meg could see Alison hesitate before she blurted out the truth. "Chuck found him for me. Lucky's not just good-looking. You should see him race around the barrels. We've won three races this year—"

Jesse broke in. "Chuck must be a good buddy to find you a horse like this." He looked down at Alison and winked, then turned to the next camper.

"What did he mean by that?" Alison hissed to Meg.

"I don't know, but here comes Becky with Shadow," Meg said, determined not to get involved. She was relieved Becky was coming on this trip. When Alison was in lovestruck mode, she was pretty useless!

"Okay, girls, mount up." Jesse put them in trail position. "Alison, you bring up the rear—make sure nobody gets too far behind. Becky you ride in the middle and, Meg, you're up front behind me."

"Can't I switch with Meg?" Alison protested. "Lucky hates being last."

"*Alison* hates being last," Becky whispered to Meg.

"We'll start out the way I said." Jesse shook his head. "If it doesn't work, we'll switch." He pushed back his hat so the girls could see his whole face. "Listen up now, Cabin 3."

The campers all stared in his direction, as if a rock star had come on stage. For once, there was no "This is bor-ing" or "Do we have to?" The girls were excited about this trip.

"We have to reach our camp at Burnt Creek by nightfall and it's a long ride," explained Jesse. "We'll take a break for lunch, and if anyone needs another break, just sing out. But before we go, I want to make sure you all know the basic rules of trail riding. Okay, let me hear 'em."

"We ride in single file," cried Dee-Dee in her high-pitched voice. "And we don't let our horse pass another horse."

"Lean forward going up hills!" Rachel's dark eyes sparkled as she shouted the rule to Jesse.

"Lean back going downhill," called Courtney.

"Take your feet out of the stirrups if the horse is on really rough ground," Jordan said.

"Keep your head down and lean forward going under tree branches," added Cam.

Becky hoisted herself into Shadow's saddle and grinned at Meg. "Wow! They *were* listening to all that stuff I taught them. I don't think we're going to have any trouble with Jesse leading this out-trip."

"Maybe not with the campers." Meg laughed. "But what about Alison?"

Like a compass seeking north, Alison had swung Lucky's nose in Jesse's direction. Meg shook her head. "I'll bet you a chocolate bar that by lunchtime today she's riding behind him and I'm at the back."

"Poor Chuck." Becky looked toward the ranch house. "He didn't even come out to say goodbye, and Alison couldn't care less!"

Jesse crossed the yard on Tailor, riding through the gate and down the green meadow to the creek that flowed at the edge of the ranch.

In single file, the others followed. They splashed through the shallow, swift-flowing water and climbed the bank on the other side, heading south.

Meg glanced up. Above them loomed the peak of Mustang Mountain and the stone horse, flaming in the morning sun. The cave in the horse's flared nostril was just a small dark shadow.

"It looks so high!" she heard Dee-Dee gasp behind her. "Will we really get way up there?"

Riding at the end of the string, Alison looked over her shoulder to see if Chuck had come out to wave them on their way. There was no sign of the tall red-headed cowboy. She felt guilty, leaving Chuck without a word. But what could she do? Chuck wasn't exciting like Jesse. This whole past year, she realized, she'd been bored. Now, seeing Jesse, it was like coming back to life. Chuck was great to be with, a friend, almost a big brother. But Jesse was like this trail ride—full of danger and excitement.

CHAPTER 8

CHAIN SAW!

Alison and Jordan quickly fell behind the other riders. Ahead of them loomed a steep slope.

"C-can we make it up there?" Jordan stammered.

"Come on! All the others made it—ages ago!" Alison urged. But Rocco stumbled and slid, lurching from one side to the other as he started up the hill.

"Go faster!" Alison shouted at Jordan. "Lucky can't climb at this pace. He needs to build up momentum."

Jordan clung for dear life to her saddle horn. Rocco scrabbled in the loose dirt.

Finally, Alison forced Lucky past them.

"But ... but you're not supposed to pass ..." Jordan's voice quavered. She was terrified that Rocco was going to slip and throw her off.

"Just lean forward and give him lots of encouragement," Alison called over her shoulder. "And for Pete's sake, quit letting him stop to eat!" She disappeared down the trail through the trees while Jordan was still trying to urge the struggling Rocco to the top.

For a while, Jordan could hear Alison and Lucky. Then the sound died away. She was surrounded by a silence so big and terrible it rang in her ears.

Rocco stopped to nibble on bushes by the trail. "STOP THAT!" Jordan tugged on his reins. "We're getting farther behind!"

The gray horse ignored her as if she were just an annoying fly on his back. Soon Jordan's hands were sore with tugging. Her arms ached from trying to lift Rocco's heavy head.

She wanted to slide from her saddle and leave him there eating leaves, but she was too scared. What if she met a grizzly bear? What if the others had branched off on another trail and she got lost? Rocco had a better chance of finding the other horses than she did—if he wanted to.

"Let's GO!" She yanked at Rocco's reins with all her strength, and this time he took a few steps forward, but only to reach the next tasty bush and rip off a mouthful of leaves. Jordan fell forward on his neck and let her hands go limp. "I can't do this," she moaned. "I wish I'd never come to this stupid camp. I thought it would be fun. I thought I would learn to ride! I thought I'd be spending two weeks with other kids who loved horses.

Instead, they're a bunch of mean bullies and crazy counselors who leave you all alone on a lazy jerk of a horse
that ... won't ... GO!"

Up ahead, Meg followed Jesse through a forest of tall
lodgepole pines. The horses' feet sank into a thick layer of
green moss and wild cranberry bushes dotted with small
pink flowers. A brisk wind blew rowdy white clouds
across a clear blue sky. The pines sang in the wind.

Behind, Meg heard the laughter and chatter of the
campers. They might not appreciate the beauty that surrounded them but at least they were having fun.

They were working their way down the ridge when
suddenly the whine of a chain saw split the air, making
the horses bolt in all directions.

Meg and Jesse rode through a screen of pines to
a cleared strip that gashed the forest like a scar. Every
single tree had been mowed down, chewed up and spat
out like a weed by a monster machine. The air smelled
of fresh wood and gasoline fumes. At the edge of the
cleared strip, a man in an orange vest and hard hat was
wielding his chain saw like a carving knife.

A huge pine crashed to the ground.

"Stop that thing!" Jesse shouted. "I've got riders
comin' through. You're spooking the horses!"

The man shut the screaming saw down to a rumbling idle and threw up the ear protectors on his hard

hat. "Sorry!" he yelled. "Didn't expect to see any riders up here. Go on through."

"I've got a bunch of kids back there. Can you shut that thing off?"

The man turned off the saw and pushed up his goggles. He pointed to where the pines, cut loose from their stumps, were caught in the branches of other trees. "I got to cut these trees that are hung up before they fall and kill somebody. The clear-cutting crew came through a few days ago. I'm just cleanin' up after them."

"Why are you clear-cutting?" Meg asked.

"For an oil pipeline." The man stuck out his hand to Jesse. "The name's George. I work for Power Pipelines."

"Jesse." Jesse shook his outstretched hand. George had a sunburned face except for where the goggles had made white circles around his eyes.

He looked curiously at Meg and Jesse. "What are you folks doin' outside the wildlife protection area?"

"We're taking a bunch of kids to the top of Mustang Mountain," Jesse explained. "This is the easiest route."

By this time, Alison and the campers had joined them. They stared at the devastation made by the clear-cutting.

"Wow! What a mess." Rachel shook her head. "What are you doing? Building a four-lane highway?"

"Nope. Just an oil pipeline." George grinned.

"This whole area is going to be developed by oil and gas companies," Cam remarked. "I heard my dad say so."

"Cam never lets us forget her dad's a big shot," Courtney mumbled loud enough for Cam to hear.

"That's not true!" Cam's face turned red. "I just hear stuff—"

Poor Cam, thought Meg. It can't be easy being a cabinet minister's daughter.

At the same time, Meg's heart sank at Cam's news. No wonder they were thinking of closing Mustang Mountain Ranch. This was prime oil and gas exploration territory. How long could it be preserved for training horses and protecting wild creatures?

George set down his heavy saw. "If you're headin' around the mountain, I'd be careful," he told them. "Our crew has reported bridges out and roads closed on account of all that rain we had last week."

"We'll be takin' higher trails and keepin' clear of roads," Jesse assured him. "Should be able to stay out of trouble."

"Well, if you're goin' way up there, watch out for mud slides." George shook his head. "You never know what the rain might have loosened. I used to work for the avalanche patrol in these mountains. There's such a thing as a mud avalanche, too, you know."

"We'll be careful," Jesse promised. "If you give us ten minutes, we'll get the horses across the clear-cut and you can get back to work."

"It might be longer than that," Alison said nervously. "I lost Jordan back there."

Meg stared at the circle of campers on horseback.

Why hadn't she noticed that Jordan was missing?

Jesse shot Alison a disappointed look. "You were supposed to be lookin' after the kid!"

"Don't blame Alley Cat," Courtney snorted. "If we went at Jordan's speed, we wouldn't get to our camp till two o'clock in the morning."

"Jordan's the queen of slowpokes," Dee-Dee agreed.

"Doesn't matter," said Jesse, shoving his hat farther down his forehead. "Alison, Becky, you'd better go back and look for her." He turned to George. "Sorry, buddy, this might take awhile."

"I'll wait till I see you all get across," George promised. "So long as it's not too long."

Ten minutes later, Jordan was bouncing along on a jogging Rocco with Alison riding ahead and Becky behind.

Rocco was annoyed that he couldn't stop to eat. He chose a route that bumped Jordan's legs against tree trunks and scraped her under low branches.

"Duck!" Becky roared as Rocco raced under a pine tree.

The pine bough scraped across the top of Jordan's helmet.

"Don't let him get away with that stuff!" Alison shouted. "It could take your head off."

"I'm trying," wailed Jordan, "but how do I stop him?"

Jordan needed more riding lessons, Becky could see.

Her reins were so loose she had to haul with all her force to make any contact with Rocco's mouth, and her feet flopped at his sides.

It was no surprise the horse had no respect for the girl on his back and was infuriated by her constant yanking. Jordan was going to have an awful three days unless things changed.

There was a stony silence as the three rode up to the pipeline clear-cut.

"Let's move on!" Jesse urged, finally. "We still have a long way to ride to our lunch stop."

"Can't we take a rest here?" Jordan panted. She was dying to get off Rocco's back.

"A *rest*?" Cam raised her fair eyebrows. "We've been hanging around here for half an hour doing nothing already!"

"But I haven't." Jordan slumped forward in her saddle. She felt sick, she was so tired. Every part of her body hurt, from her ankles, twisted at an unnatural angle in the stirrups, to her bruised legs, aching shoulders and stinging hands.

"Everybody off their horse and into your rain gear," Becky ordered. "It looks like we might get rained on."

"Oh, come on! You're just trying to find an excuse for Jordan to rest!" Rachel said. "I thought that chain saw guy was in a hurry for us to cross this clearing."

Becky pointed at the sky. "See that?" One of the clouds racing over the mountains had a dark gray bottom. High in the air, she could see wisps of rain blowing their way.

The campers dismounted, untied the rolled-up rain slickers behind their saddles and shrugged into them.

"Look! This is ridiculous!" Dee-Dee giggled. Her long yellow raincoat reached the ground. It flapped around her like a yellow sail.

"We don't usually get ranch hands that short." Becky grinned at her. "Come on, let me help you up on Cloudy."

The raincoat was split up the back and the sides hung far below Dee-Dee's stirrups. "At least you'll be dry," said Becky. "Everybody else okay?"

Meanwhile, Meg had been helping Jordan, whose fingers were too stiff to loosen the cord that tied her coat to the saddle.

"Stretch while you have a chance," Meg whispered to the weary-looking girl.

"I don't know if I can get on Rocco again," Jordan whispered back. "He won't do anything I tell him."

Meg stroked Rocco's muscled neck—he was full of tension and resistance—and made a quick decision.

"It's all right. Ride Cody for a while. He's a big softie. I'll ride Rocco."

Becky walked over. "Good idea. And don't pull on the reins unless you want Cody to stop," she instructed Jordan in a low voice. "Keep your hands relaxed. He'll know what to do."

"Are you sure?" Jordan looked doubtful. "Then I won't really be riding him, will I?"

"It's different on a trail ride like this," Becky said. "The horses follow one another."

She could see Jordan's slender shoulders sag with relief. She helped her into Cody's saddle and adjusted the stirrups. "I'll ride behind her," she suggested to Meg. "You ride Rocco in front. That way we won't lose her."

"Are we finally going?" Cam called. All the others were mounted in a line, with Alison riding right behind Jesse, as Meg had predicted.

As they started across the cleared strip, Rocco snorted and stamped, but feeling Meg's quiet confidence and soft, sure hands on the reins, he soon settled into the shuffling walk of the trail. Behind them, they heard the roar of George's chain saw start again.

CHAPTER 9

CRACKED BONES

Before the lunch break, they rode along the side of a sheltered valley. The trail was easier for the horses here, with firmer ground and more open country. The dark clouds soon blew over, and the riders took off their rain gear and tied it behind their saddles.

Alison, riding with Jesse ahead of the others, was trying to work out a way to win back his respect.

All right, I messed up, she admitted to herself. I wanted to catch up to Jesse—but I should have stayed with Jordan. She's the youngest, and the others all pick on her, but honestly, she asks for it. She's so *hopeless* on a horse!

She glanced at Jesse. Now *there* was a great rider, so natural in the saddle that he seemed part of his horse. Straight back, well-balanced, moving in rhythm to Tailor's gait—he was perfect—so perfect!

Suddenly, Jesse stopped and slipped from Tailor's saddle. He was staring at something in the long grass.

"What is it?" Alison rode close.

Jesse squatted on his heels. "It *was* a horse," he said slowly.

"Eee-agh!" Alison choked. All that was left of the horse were its hooves, its rib cage and the long black hair of its mane and tail. "What happened to it?"

"Well, I don't think it died of old age." Jesse examined one of the hooves. "Too bad. Judging by this, it was a wild horse—tough hoof, never been shod."

"A cougar?" Alison gasped the question. Two years before, they had lost a trail horse to a cougar that jumped on him from a high ledge.

Jesse looked closely at the rib bones. "Don't think so. These ribs have been cracked to get at the marrow. Only wolves do that."

"Can wolves kill a horse?" Alison asked in surprise.

"A wolf can take down a horse, easy." Jesse nodded. "They go for the tendons in the back of his legs and hamstring 'em. Some people say they eat their prey alive."

Alison shuddered at the thought. The long strands of horsehair and the cracked bones told a bleak story of an animal fighting for its life against a fierce predator. And here it lay in this peaceful place among the wild roses and grass, with the wind whispering through the poplars.

She looked up to see Jesse studying her face. "You're not as spiky and tough as you pretend to be, are you, Al?" he said gently.

"Do I seem—spiky—to you?"

"Sometimes." Jesse looked away. "Here comes the rest of the bunch. If I were you, I'd keep quiet about the wolves. Don't want to scare the kids."

"Do you think there are still wolves around?"

"Might be." Jesse straightened up and reached for Tailor's reins. With one swift motion he was back in his saddle.

The campers surrounded the skeleton. "What's that?" gasped Dee-Dee, pointing to the bones and hair.

"Just the bones of a horse." Jesse winked at Alison. "It probably died of old age."

"Jesse thinks it might have been a wild horse," Alison told Meg. "He can tell by its hooves."

Meg looked down at the horse's scattered remains. "Poor thing! I'll have to tell Thomas when he comes. He'll want to see this and figure out what happened—" she paused, "*if* he comes."

Alison was on the verge of telling Meg what Jesse had said about the wolves and the cracked bones, but she decided to wait until they were alone. Jesse was right. The kids might overhear and not be keen on camping out for the night with a pack of hungry wolves.

At two o'clock they took a short lunch break on the side of the valley, not far from the horse's skeleton.

"It takes my appetite away, thinking of those horrible bones." Dee-Dee made a face.

"Nothing takes my appetite away," mumbled Courtney, stuffing cheese and crackers into her large mouth. "I could eat a horse! Oh! Sorry, Dee-Dee."

"That's because you're growing into a giant," sighed Rachel. "I wish I was tall like you, Courtney. If I ate like that, I'd be a blimp."

Cam stood up, crumpling her sandwich wrapper. "Hurry up and finish. We're never going to reach the stone horse at this rate."

Rachel stared at her. "Tell me something. What is it with you and this trophy hunt? Why are you so obsessed?"

"I want to find the jade in the cave." Cam flushed angrily. "I thought we all did."

"We do but—" Rachel shrugged, "do you have to remind us every five minutes?"

Jesse interrupted. "Don't forget to take all your garbage with you," he reminded them. "Pack it in your empty lunch bag."

"Yes, master." Rachel threw him an adoring look. "We in Cabin 3 obey your command."

Jesse shoved his hat down over his dark blue eyes and strode to his horse.

"You embarrass him when you talk like that," Alison scolded her.

"I know, but isn't he adorable?" sighed Rachel.

Meg was watching Cam. Her face had lost its angry flush, but it was clear from her impatient jerk on Spencer's reins that she was frustrated at their slow pace.

"Rachel's right," Meg murmured to Becky and Alison as they stowed their garbage and got ready to ride. "This trophy hunt is almost an obsession with Cam."

"The question is, why?" Becky asked as she swung into Shadow's saddle.

"Maybe she just loves pretty stones." Alison leaped aboard Lucky. "Does it matter? If we keep Cam happy, we're helping save the ranch. Isn't that the point?"

"I guess so." Becky watched the campers fall into line. "As long as we can get to the stone horse without taking too many risks. It wasn't old age that killed that horse, was it?"

After lunch, their trail led them to the base of Mustang Mountain itself. Soon they came to the first sign of mud slides caused by the rain. The path wound under a high cliff, and rocks had fallen from its top, blocking their way.

"Do you think we can get around those big chunks of rock?" Becky rode up to consult with Jesse.

Jesse scanned the cliff face. "It's not the rocks that have already fallen that bother me," he grunted. "It's the ones that are going to fall. I don't like the look of that cliff."

As if to answer, a small shower of loose gravel skittered down in front of them.

"I see your point." Becky frowned. "So what do you suggest?"

"Backtrack to the last junction," said Jesse, "and take the trail up across the top of this cliff. It's harder for the horses, but safer." He glanced at his watch. "It's already three-thirty. We'll have to hurry if we're going to make camp tonight."

The trail across the top of the cliff turned out to be much harder, and not just for the horses.

Here, close to the timberline, the trees were far apart and stunted, bent by the wind into twisted shapes. With no shade, the sun blasted down. The horses' hides were soon dark with sweat.

"Can we really get to Burnt Creek Camp this way?" Alison called forward to Jesse.

"Yup." Jesse nodded. "If we don't have any more holdups."

Alison could hear the tension in his voice. She turned in her saddle to check the other riders.

Their giggles and chattering had stopped as they rode up the tough trail. Their horses, used to rocky terrain, stepped carefully and swished their tails. Becky and Meg were still riding in front of and behind Jordan.

Twenty minutes later, Jesse held his arm up for another halt. "We're back in the wildlife protection area," he announced as the other riders clustered around him. "We shouldn't hear any more chain saws or see any clear-cutting from here on."

"How much farther to Burnt Creek Camp?" Cam called out the question that was on all the campers' minds. None of them had ever been on such a long ride.

"Another four hours or so," Jesse told them.

"Ohhh!" groaned Rachel. "I'll never make it. My knees feel like they've been twisted into pretzels!"

"This trail is so rough," added Courtney. "I hate it."

Jesse looked at her long body, flopped forward on her horse's neck. "Listen up," he said. "The whole day tomorrow will be ridin' like this—rocky and a lot of it above the tree line. It's a hard climb to the stone horse and back down to the camp again. But you don't have to make that your destination. We can take an easier trip—"

"No!" Cam sat up straight. "We're going to the stone horse," she blurted out. "We're going after the jade trophy."

"Is that a unanimous decision?" Becky looked closely at the campers' tired faces. It was time to decide if this was just Cam's idea, or something that mattered to all the girls.

Rachel raised her eyebrows. "I guess so."

Courtney shoved her glasses up her nose. "It can't be much worse than this."

Dee-Dee shrugged. "I hate to give up now."

Jordan just nodded.

"All right," Jesse said, urging Tailor forward. "But no more complaints about the trail. If we make time, we should reach the camp well before dark."

Meg, taking her place at the end of the line of horses, was relieved they were back in the wildlife protection zone. She hadn't mentioned it to anyone, but she'd seen stud piles along the trail. These pyramids of stallion dung were a sure sign that wild horses used this path. The stallions always pooped in the same place as a marker for other horses, and some of the piles had fresh manure on top. If the horses were in a protected area, they'd be safer from hunters, Meg knew.

There was another reason those piles of stallion poop made her happy. If wild horses were in the area, maybe Thomas was tracking them. Maybe he was somewhere close by. Maybe he'd even got her note and would be waiting for them at Burnt Creek Camp!

CHAPTER 10

SURPRISE GUESTS

There was no sign of Thomas when, more than four hours later, an exhausted finally crew climbed off their horses at Burnt Creek Camp. The little creek flowed through a grove of trees bordered by a high mountain meadow.

"Before you collapse," Meg called out the order, "take off your saddles and bridles and lead the horses to the creek to drink."

"But I'm sooo tired," moaned Dee-Dee.

"I thought we'd be able to rest when we got here," Rachel whined.

"This is where we have to sleep?" Cam looked around the campground in disbelief. "No building, not even an outhouse?"

"That's your outhouse." Becky pointed to a blue tarp stretched around four poles.

"What kind of camp is this?" Courtney glared from under her straight black bangs.

"A wilderness camp!" Becky exploded. "What did you expect—a five-star hotel?"

"Think of your horses before yourselves," Meg insisted. "They got you here, and they'll get you back to the ranch—if you look after them."

The campers rolled their eyes at her.

"All right, Meg the Nag," Rachel muttered, and a couple of the others snorted under their breath.

So they had found a nickname for her now, too. I'm a nag, am I? Meg thought. The name stung but it didn't matter, as long as they started unbuckling those cinches!

While Jesse, Alison and Becky unloaded the packhorse and started setting up camp, Meg led Rocco, the campers and all their horses to the creek.

It was a small stream, trickling from a high mountain spring, and the water was ice cold. The sky was still light, but the sun had slipped behind the mountains to the west. It would be dark in a few more hours.

Meg wondered about the wolves Alison had told them about while they were riding. Had they left the wolf pack behind at the lower altitudes, or was Burnt Creek part of their range? They'd soon know.

In the meantime, there were horses and people to feed.

Jesse had chosen Burnt Creek because it had a high

meadow with rich grass. The horses could be turned loose with large bells around their necks to graze all night.

"All right, campers," Meg called, "once your horses have been watered, lead them back to Jesse. He'll show you what to do next. But don't be too long—I need you all to help me find firewood. No fire—no dinner."

More groans greeted this order. The campers were drooping with weariness. But once they'd seen to the horses, they straggled back to look for wood.

Meg made sure Jordan wasn't straggling behind as they headed for the sparse grove of trees. This was grizzly bear country, and no one should be alone.

A fire had swept through the area years before, giving Burnt Creek its name. "Look for old logs that are partly burned," Meg called out. "They're good firewood. Also small stuff—twigs and little branches. We need that for kindling."

The girls scattered. Meg noticed that Courtney, Rachel and Dee-Dee stayed close together, giggling and laughing and turning the task into a game. Jordan and Cam stayed apart, working quietly, and they brought back most of the wood. The difference was that Jordan looked longingly at the three who were having all the fun, while Cam stayed aloof.

"And now, while I'm cooking you a delicious dinner," Meg told them as they dumped their armloads of wood beside the camp's firepit, "you need to set up your tent and make your beds. C'mon—let's go! The sooner you get those beds made, the sooner you can drop into them."

She quickly had a roaring fire going, with a blackened coffeepot steaming between two flaming logs. Meg would use the water to make hot chocolate for everyone. Baked beans simmered in another pot and sausages sizzled in a frying pan. For dessert there was apple crisp.

While she cooked, Meg listened to the five campers arguing in their tent. Even from a distance, she could hear their voices raised over who was sleeping next to whom. Jordan, she'd be willing to bet, would have the lumpiest spot of ground under her sleeping bag. She wished there was more she could do to help her without obviously playing favorites.

All at once she heard Jesse call, "We've got company."

"Thomas!" Meg whispered to herself, straightening.

But it wasn't Thomas. Two men on horseback rode up to the camp. They sat on their horses, looking down at the fire and the food cooking. One was older, on a brown horse with a white sock. The other man looked younger and rode a paint.

"Hello there," said the younger man.

Jesse, Alison and Becky appeared from the grove of trees where they'd been feeding and grooming the horses.

"Howdy," Jesse said, giving a nod.

Meg was on the point of asking the two visitors to share dinner with them when Jesse shot her a warning look. What were these guys doing there, halfway up Mustang Mountain?

Finally, Alison spoke up. "We're from a riding camp down below," she told the men. "We've got five kids on an out-trip."

"Going higher?" the larger and older of the two men asked.

Becky took a step forward. "How about you guys?" she shot in, brushing back a strand of her fair hair. "What are you doing up this way?"

"Just checking out the scenery," the older man said. "When we saw your fire, we thought you might be the fella who's been tailing us—some Native guy on an Appaloosa."

Meg sucked in her breath. *Thomas!* He was close and had been tailing these two men for some reason. She exchanged a startled glance with Becky.

"What makes you think he's—" Alison started to ask.

"Don't be so nosy!" Meg broke in. "I'm sure these men have somewhere they have to be."

The younger man gave her a crooked grin. "Yeah, let's go, Bruce. Let these people have their supper. I get the feelin' we're interrupting."

The older man swung his horse away from the fire. "Okay then, folks. We'll be on our way. You have yourselves a good dinner."

They rode off at a jog.

"Meg!" Alison hissed, "he must have been talking about Thomas. Why would he be following *those* guys?"

"Well, whatever his reason, I'm sure Thomas wants to keep it a secret." Becky shook her head.

"I wasn't going to ..." Alison protested.

Jesse was watching the men ride away. "One rides a brown horse, and the other rides a paint," he muttered. "Remember that."

"Why?!" Alison looked ready to stamp with impatience.

"Because Jesse thinks there's something funny about Bruce and his friend, and so do I." Becky turned on her. "Don't they remind you of somebody, Alison? That bounty hunter we ran into a couple of years ago, for instance?"

"Or the wild horse rustlers I met last summer," Meg murmured. "Maybe they're after wild horses, and that's why Thomas is tracking them. He could be in danger!"

"Now, don't go imaginin' things," Jesse warned. "They're probably not bounty hunters or rustlers. All the same, I'm glad the kids are in their tent and didn't come buzzin' around asking questions."

"Or telling them where we're headed tomorrow," Becky agreed.

Jesse was still staring off in the direction the two men had disappeared. "I think I'll ride after those two, keep out of sight, but just see where they're headed," he said.

"Can I come with you?" Alison begged.

"I'd rather you didn't, Al." Jesse shook his head. "Those fellas are more likely to notice two horses than one." He started back to where Tailor was tied to a line strung between two trees.

Alison stood looking after him, her hands on her hips. "He still treats me like I'm a kid," she said sorrowfully.

"Well, maybe if you weren't so obvious." Becky grinned. "Remember what you said about Chuck? No one likes an overanxious puppy trailing at their heels."

"Chuck ...?" Alison murmured. "I haven't thought about him since this morning."

"Meg! Your beans are burning!" Becky dove for the pot and jumped back as she touched the hot handle.

"Let me ..." Meg grabbed a towel to wrap around her hand. She'd been standing in a trance, thinking about Thomas—so near. She stirred the beans fiercely, scraping the burnt ones from the bottom.

"Here come the campers," warned Alison. "Brace yourselves."

CHAPTER 11

TAPS

But the four campers were a bedraggled bunch as they gathered around the fire. Rachel's eyes had lost their challenging gleam. Cam's knot of blonde hair had come undone and straggled down her back. Courtney looked like a tall bag of bones held up by willpower alone, and Dee-Dee whimpered like a lost kitten. "I'll never be able to eat. I'm sooo ex*haus*ted!"

"Where's Jordan?" asked Meg, peering toward their tent.

"Still making her bed." Rachel waved a weary hand. "The zipper on her sleeping bag was stuck, or something."

"And of course none of you helped her!" Alison glared at them.

"You don't know what it's like," sighed Courtney. "She's so slow at whatever she does, or she's just off on her own agenda, doing her own thing."

"I've had it with her," Dee-Dee announced. "I'm smaller than she is, and I keep up!"

"I'll go and give her a hand," Meg muttered.

"So! We all have to wait to eat now?" Rachel exclaimed. "Because of Jordan?"

"We should wait for Jesse anyhow." Becky nearly growled the words at her. "That would only be polite."

"Where *is* the mighty cowboy?" asked Rachel.

"Gone to check the horses," Becky lied. No use getting these kids fired up about a visit from two mysterious strangers. Not that it would worry this bunch. They seemed totally fixated on their own sorry selves!

Meg found Jordan sound asleep on her sleeping bag.

"Wake up," Meg called gently. "Food's almost ready."

"Oh!" Jordan sat bolt upright, a look of terror on her face. "Oh—I had the most awful dream. I dreamed that rocks were falling on me and Cody, and we were going to be crushed into the side of the mountain, and all that would be left of us was cracked bones."

"Just a dream." Meg wanted to reach out and brush back the wisp of fine hair that fell over Jordan's frightened eyes. The poor kid, she thought. "You did really well today," she told her, helping her to her feet. "Once you got on Cody, you rode much better, and you kept up with the others. I'm proud of you."

A grin spread across Jordan's thin face. "Whew! I guess I did. Where is everybody? How long have I been sleeping?"

"Not long." Meg smiled. "We're all sitting around the fire, waiting for Jesse. Here, let me help you with your sleeping bag before it gets too dark in here to see."

In a few minutes, Meg had the zipper on Jordan's bag fixed. "Is this your spot?" she asked, feeling around the lumpy ground.

"Yeah. It's not the best, but at least I'm sleeping beside Dee-Dee and not Courtney," sighed Jordan. "She's got a tongue like a mean cat." She frowned. "Would I ever like to show those guys ..."

She didn't finish, but Meg knew what she meant. Show them that she wasn't a pathetic baby, that she could hold her own on this out-trip. That she could ride.

"C'mon," Meg urged. "You'll feel a lot better once you get some food in you."

As they walked back to the firepit, Meg saw that Jesse had returned.

Full of sausages, beans and apple crisp, the campers and counselors sat close around the fire as dusk gathered in.

"You kids know any camp songs?" Jesse asked into the silence.

There were only grunts from the tired campers. They were almost asleep.

"We always used to sing around the campfire when I was a kid," Jesse went on. "Know this one?"

He began to sing softly:

"Fire's burning, fire's burning,
Draw nearer, draw nearer,
In the gloaming, in the gloaming,
Come sing and be merry."

"What the heck is 'the gloaming'?" Dee-Dee interrupted.

"It's a twilight glow in the sky, like now." Jesse pointed to the pink and purple sky over the mountains. "Come on, we sing the song in a round. Alison and I will start, then Meg and Becky, then you five."

He and Alison started to sing, "Fire's burning, fire's burning ..."

Meg and Becky joined in after the first line. Would the campers sing? Becky wondered.

Sure enough, creaky and ragged at first, but with more confidence, the kids took up the song. They all finished with a rousing "Come sing and be merry!"

"Great!" Jesse nodded with a grin. "Know any more?"

"How about 'Home on the Range'?" Dee-Dee piped up.

Meg got up and filled everyone's mug with hot chocolate from the coffeepot in the coals as the singing started. Becky threw more wood on the fire.

"This is more like it," Rachel sighed when the song was over. "I'm full and warm and I'm *not* on a horse."

"I can't believe we rode all the way up here," Dee-Dee chimed in.

"My dad will never believe I could do it," murmured Cam.

"Let's sing another song," suggested Courtney. "How about 'Blood on the Saddle'?"

As the campers roared verse after verse of the old cowboy song, Jesse leaned over to mutter in Alison's ear. "I'm glad they're singing. I'd like whoever, or whatever, is out there to think there are a lot of people in this camp tonight."

"What did you see while you were out there following Bruce and the other guy?" Alison whispered back. Tingles ran up her back. Jesse was so close she could smell the warm, old leather of his vest.

"They're camped not too far from here," Jesse told her. "And they have high-powered rifles with them. Not your usual equipment for lookin' at the scenery."

"You said 'whatever,' too," Alison reminded him. "What else is out there?"

"I saw a pair of wolves on the ridge just above us." Jesse stirred the fire with a stick.

"Just two little wolves?" Alison gulped. "Well, that's better than a grizzly bear, isn't it?"

"They're not likely to give us any trouble," Jesse agreed. "Wolves don't attack people, especially with a fire. Still, I think it would be better not to mention it to the kids. Once it's dark, I'll bring the horses in from the meadow. They've had a good turnout by now."

He stood up. "I hate to interrupt this great singsong, but the sun's down—time for Taps. Everybody know it?"

"We should." Rachel beamed. "We sing it every night at campfire." The five girls struggled stiffly to their feet and formed a circle around the fire, each reaching for the hand of the person next to her. Their happy faces glowed in the firelight.

They look like different kids, Meg thought. Satisfied. Proud of themselves.

Alison held Jesse's hand and felt the tingle run through her again. The old song lifted into the night:

"Day is done,

Gone the sun

From the lake, from the hills, from the sky.

All is well, safely rest ..."

Safely rest? Alison wondered. She hoped so! As the campers straggled toward their tent, Jesse left quietly to round up the horses. It might be a long night.

CHAPTER 12

NIGHT OF THE WOLVES

At midnight, on her way back from the makeshift out-house, Becky glimpsed yellow eyes gleaming in the darkness just off to her right. Fierce, slanted, unblinking eyes.

When she shone her flashlight sharply in their direction, the eyes vanished. Becky hurried to the tent. She unzipped the door and threw herself in between Alison and Meg.

"Ouch! What are you doing?" Alison sat up.

"Quick. Zip the door. There are animals out there."

Alison zipped the tent shut. "I know. Jesse saw two wolves on the ridge above the meadow." She squirmed back into her sleeping bag.

Just then a long low howl echoed through the night.

It sounded far away, but the answering howl, when it came, was closer.

"Wolves—at least two—maybe more." Becky shuddered. Just then, another piercing cry filled the night, this one even closer.

"Ahhh-oooo!"

Meg jerked bolt upright. "It sounds like they're circling the camp."

"I'd better go and see if the girls are all right." Alison pulled on her boots. "They must be scared."

"The kids are probably asleep—you're just looking for an excuse to go out and see if Jesse's up!" snorted Becky.

"I am not!" Alison hissed. "I'm trying to be a responsible counselor."

The howling came again. It seemed to echo through their bones, the saddest, most mournful sound they had ever heard.

Meg could hear the horses moving restlessly in their temporary rope pen. "The horses don't like it," she muttered, reaching for her own boots. "I'll see if I can settle them down."

"Well, I'm not staying here by myself," Becky grumbled. "Can't sleep anyway with that noise."

The three of them squirmed out the tent door, flashlights in hand. Sure enough, Jesse's tall figure was lit by the fire as he threw in large branches to make it blaze higher.

"I'll help!" Alison ran to join him.

"So much for the responsible counselor," Meg whispered to Becky. "If you check the kids, I'll see to the horses."

Becky swished through the grass to the campers' tent. She knelt and gently unzipped the door. "Everybody okay in here?" she called softly.

Five snores answered.

"Thought so." Becky grinned to herself in the darkness. "Those kids are so tired they could sleep through a stampede."

Meanwhile Meg had slipped under the rope to the horses. "Steady, guys," she crooned. "It's just howling. The wolves can't get you. You're safe in here, all together, with all of us standing guard."

She went back and joined the others at the campfire.

"Listen to them!" Alison shivered. "It sounds like they've surrounded us. Maybe they're the same wolves that killed that wild horse we found."

"The howling is just the pack calling to one another," Jesse assured them. "Like us singin' camp songs. Don't worry—they're not after us. I like the sound, myself."

"Just the same, I hope Thomas isn't out there alone." Meg shivered. "I was sure he would have turned up by now."

"So that Native guy those two men were talking about is your friend Thomas?" asked Jesse. "The guy I'm replacing on this trip?"

"We're all friends with Thomas," Becky corrected. "But he's Meg's boyfriend."

"He wants to start a refuge for wild horses," Alison added. "He's crazy about them."

Meg could feel herself blush in the darkness. She took a large branch and threw it on the fire. She knew what Jesse must be thinking. If Thomas was in the area, why wasn't he guiding this trip like he was supposed to? It was a good question!

It was almost three in the morning before the wolf chorus died away in the distance.

"Sounds like the hunt's over," Jesse yawned. "How about some shut-eye?"

They crawled back into their tents—Jesse into his one-person backpacker's tent and Meg, Alison and Becky into their crowded three-person pop-up.

"It's no use going back to sleep," Becky groaned. "We'll be up in three hours."

"I can feel every stick and pebble under this sleeping bag," Meg agreed.

Alison sighed. "Just two layers of thin nylon between me and Jesse. He feels so near ..."

"Will you give it a rest?!" Becky reached over and thumped the lump that was Alison's sleeping bag.

Alison raised herself on one elbow. "I think he really likes me," she whispered excitedly.

"You're dreaming," Becky scoffed. "He just tolerates you, that's all."

"No ... really!" Alison shook Becky's shoulder. "When we were sitting by the fire just now, he kept looking over at me."

"That's because you were doing everything you could to get his attention except burst into flames!" Becky shot back. "Asking him every ten minutes if he wanted more coffee, fanning the smoke out of his eyes, making a major production out of every twig you put on the fire— Oh! Eee! That one almost burned me!" Becky imitated Alison's voice.

"Be quiet!" Alison shoved her arm again. "He'll hear you."

"He probably already has and wishes we would shut up and let him sleep," Becky chuckled. "Good night, Alison. Good night, Meg."

"Good night," murmured Meg. She had been wiggling around, trying to find a comfortable position on the lumpy ground.

If I were a wolf, she thought, I'd climb the highest hill and howl for Thomas. How am I ever going to find him in this wilderness?

Meg shot out of bed the next morning to the sound of shouts, squeals and laughter.

Without boots on, her feet icy in the cold dew, she took a few steps from the tent door and stopped short.

"What are you doing?" she shrieked.

Four girls in pajamas were dancing around a collapsed tent that was wriggling and thrashing like a wild beast.

Muffled cries came from inside. "Let me out! Help! I can't breathe!"

Meg dashed to the tent. "What have you done?" She grabbed Rachel's arm.

"Nothing!" Rachel twisted away. She was laughing so hard that tears poured down her cheeks.

"Honestly!" Courtney protested. "She did it all by herself."

Dee-Dee giggled. "*Totally* by herself. She just knocked against the center pole and down it came."

"We were all outside, minding our own business," added Cam. "Jordan was sleeping in. Late, as usual."

"And you four haven't done a thing to help her!" Meg was so mad she could practically feel steam coming out of her ears.

She was focused so firmly on the thrashing tent that she didn't hear the hoofbeats of an approaching horse or see anything until a strong hand reached down, grabbed the top of the tent and yanked it upright.

"Can I help?" asked a much loved voice. Meg looked up to see Thomas on Palouse, smiling at her.

The four campers were suddenly as still and silent as if they'd turned to stone. They stood with their mouths open, staring at the young man on the brown and white spotted horse. Thomas had jet black hair in a braid that fell over his shoulder, and as he bent to hold the top of the tent, his brown eyes looked only at Meg. His smile was only for her.

Jordan, red-faced and weeping, wriggled out of the tent. She stopped crying when she clapped eyes on Thomas.

"Don't worry." He shifted his smile from Meg to Jordan. "I've pulled my tent down on myself lots of times. Usually, it's just my horse, Palouse, who gets to laugh at me." He stroked Palouse's neck with his other hand. Thomas sat on his horse as if the two of them were one being. They made an unforgettable picture.

"I—I—I was d-dreaming again," Jordan stammered. "I thought I was falling. I grabbed for a tree branch to save me. Everything came down around my head!"

Thomas slipped from Palouse's back and took Meg's hand. "Glad I arrived in time to be some use. Sorry I'm so late." He turned his gaze back to Jordan. "These must be the Mustang Mountain Ranch campers."

Meg nodded. "Thomas, this is Jordan, and Dee-Dee, and Courtney, and Rachel, and Cam." She pointed to each of the girls. She was surprised she could even speak.

"Are you ... are you the Thomas who was supposed to be our wrangler on this trip?" Dee-Dee choked.

He nodded.

"Wow," Dee-Dee sighed. "Cool."

"Are you going to come with us on the rest of our trip?" Rachel asked.

"If Meg wants me?" Thomas's smile was teasing.

"Even if she doesn't, we do," Courtney said eagerly. "Don't we?"

There was a loud chorus of "Yes!"

"We thought Jesse was dreamy," Dee-Dee gushed. "But he's yesterday's mashed potatoes compared to you."

"Dee-Dee!" the others groaned.

"We're riding up to the nose of the stone horse on Mustang Mountain to get a trophy from the cave," Cam spoke up. "A piece of jade—there's a legend that there's jade in the horse's nostril. Do you think it's true?"

Thomas's mouth twitched with amusement. "Maybe," he said solemnly, "but I can't say I've ever heard that legend."

"Girls, why don't you put this tent back together while Thomas sees to Palouse." Meg gulped. "Then I'll make breakfast. We need to get moving if we have any hope of making it to the top of Mustang Mountain and back here tonight."

"We hear and obey, Meg the Nag," sang out Rachel. "But shouldn't you put on some clothes first?"

Meg looked down at her sock feet and baggy old pajama bottoms. She realized that her long brown hair, usually tied in a neat ponytail, was loose around her face. What a way for Thomas to see her after a year apart!

"Uh ... good idea." She hitched up her pajamas and turned away to hide her embarrassment. "See you all at the campfire in ten minutes."

"Can Jordan give me a hand with Palouse?" Thomas asked. "She owes me a favor."

Meg glanced at Jordan. "Good idea." At Thomas's suggestion, Jordan's tear-stained face brightened like the sky after a storm. The rest of the campers were staring at Thomas and Jordan with looks that ranged from wistful to jealous.

By this time, Becky and Alison had dressed and were running toward them. Jesse strode behind, a broad smile on his face.

"Thomas Horne!" Alison cried. "Where have you been?"

"Never mind that—we're so glad to see you!" Becky gave Thomas a quick hug. "Thomas, this is our friend Jesse." She turned to introduce them.

The two shook hands.

Meg was longing to hug Thomas, too, but that would have to wait for a more private moment. "He just rode in like a white knight to Jordan's rescue ..." she started to say, then caught the glimmer of laughter in Thomas's brown eyes.

"I mean, he swooped down like an eagle from the heights," she corrected herself, stroking the eagle feather Thomas had braided into Palouse's mane. Suddenly she remembered she was still in her pajamas. "Got to go get dressed!"

Her feet danced as she ran to the tent. Now that Thomas was here, nothing else really mattered!

CHAPTER 13

PLAYING TRICKS

Meg made them all a hurried breakfast of scrambled eggs and bacon, with fried bread and tea.

"It's not very healthy, is it?" Rachel growled at the greasy food.

"Better not complain," Dee-Dee sang out. "Remember what Meg said—anyone who doesn't like the food ends up doing all the cooking!"

"I'm not complaining." Rachel munched on a piece of delicious crispy bread. "I just said it wasn't good for you—not that I didn't *like* it."

"Don't worry," Jesse told her. "You'll work off every calorie getting to the stone horse. Everybody eat up. We won't have a lot of time to refuel during the climb."

He'd been awake even earlier than the others, turning the horses out to the meadow to graze.

At Jesse's order to eat up, Jordan, who'd been playing with her food, tried to hurry. She dumped her eggs onto her piece of bread and folded it in half to make a sandwich. Meg watched her chomp into it, her cheeks puffing out into two balls.

Meg was sure Jordan would gag, but she chewed till her eyes were popping, then gulped it down. The kid is trying her best, Meg thought. She doesn't deserve the treatment she's getting from the girls.

"Go and pack," she told them. "We'll leave our camping gear and most of the food here because we're coming back tonight. Just take your lunch, first aid kit, lots of water and a change of socks. The rule for today is travel light. We're heading for the heights!"

The five girls dashed for their tent.

Jesse hurried to round up the horses from the meadow.

Alison waited until they were all out of earshot, and it was just her, Becky, Thomas and Meg at the firepit.

"Where were you, Thomas Horne, when you should have been at Mustang Mountain Ranch?" she asked him pointedly.

Thomas looked up, his second plate of eggs and bacon balanced on his knee, a coffee mug in his hand.

Meg stopped scraping plates to listen. She hadn't had a chance to talk to Thomas alone and she wanted to hear this.

"I guess you heard the wolves last night." Thomas frowned. "I've been following a small band of wild horses. The wolves have been following them, too. The band had four new foals this spring. The wolves have already got one."

"The wolves killed a foal? That's awful!" Becky exclaimed.

Thomas took a swallow of coffee. "Normally there's a natural balance between wolves and their prey. The wolves only get the weak and the sick, and they keep the population down. But with the wolves being protected in the national parks, there's getting to be a lot of them, and the wild horses are under so much pressure that there's only a few left. The natural balance is upset."

He paused again. "I don't know what I can do about it, but I'd like to help this little band. They've got a good, strong stallion and a couple of nice mares."

"That still doesn't explain what you were doing following wild horses when you should have been helping us," Alison pressed him. "It's a good thing Jesse could come." She looked over to where Jesse was getting the horses ready. "He's been wonderful."

She's annoyed because the girls are making such a fuss over Thomas, Meg thought. It's as if she thinks Jesse and Thomas are rival stallions in a herd of mares. Typical Alison!

"I didn't realize you were counting on me for the camp this early," Meg heard him explain, "till I got Meg's note yesterday, when I stopped in at the ranch. But

I might have run into you anyway—the wild horse band I'm trailing came this way."

"We met a couple of riders who thought you were tailing them." Becky filled Thomas's mug from the coffeepot. "One on a brown horse, the other on a paint. Jesse said they're camped down the ridge."

Thomas nodded. "I don't know who those guys are, but I saw them on the trail, too."

Becky shook her head. "They weren't locals, for sure. We wondered if they might even be poachers."

"It's possible. There are people willing to pay big bucks for bighorn sheep and grizzly bear parts. They sell them on the black market."

"And the oil company is putting in a new pipeline ..." Meg added. "We ran across the clear-cut."

Thomas shook his head sadly. "More pressure on the horses," he said. "I'd like to get the band I'm following up to my grandfather's ranch at Rocky Mountain House. They'll be safe there, for a while." His face brightened.

Meg knew he was thinking about the wild horse refuge he'd like to set up—somewhere all the wildies could be safe.

"Well, you go ahead and follow your wild horses." Alison smiled sarcastically. "We've got Jesse."

Meg wanted to stuff a bun in Alison's smirking mouth.

Thomas stood up and handed Meg his plate. His hand gripped hers. "I'd like to ride with you today," he said softly. "The wildies are right around here and they won't move far in one day. After that ... if you don't need me ... we'll see."

Meg gulped. Maybe they didn't *need* Thomas, but so what? She wanted him. She knew the wild horses came first, but he couldn't be thinking of leaving so soon!

"I—uh—hoped you'd stay," she stammered.

"I'm glad." Thomas smiled and strode off to help Jesse with the horses.

Meg put down the plate and glared at Alison. "Did you have to say that?"

Alison shrugged. "Why not? It's the truth, isn't it?"

Becky glanced up at her. "All three of us, back together again," she sighed. "I was looking forward to it so much. You keep saying you've changed, but sometimes you seem like the same old self-centered Cousin Alison you were three years ago."

Twenty minutes later, they were on the trail. As Jesse had promised, once they left the green meadow of Burnt Creek, it climbed up over steep, rocky terrain. Jesse pressed them hard all morning.

Thomas rode in the rear, behind Jordan. She had insisted on trying to ride Rocco again, and once again, the gray horse was making her life miserable.

"What you want to do is get Rocco's attention," Thomas told her. "Next time we take a break, I'll show you a few tricks."

"That would be so great." Jordan turned in her saddle to beam at Thomas. Rocco took the opportunity to side-swipe a prickly bush.

"Ouch!" Jordan cried. "I wish he wouldn't do that!"

In the afternoon, they stopped to grab a quick lunch at a stream that gushed down the mountainside. While Jesse, Meg, Becky and Alison watered the horses, Thomas took Jordan and Rocco downstream, where there was more space to demonstrate his horse training technique, and less distraction from the other horses.

The four other campers watched them go.

"Depressing!" Dee-Dee summed up their feelings. "Why couldn't Thomas pick me for a private lesson?"

"He took Jordan because she's Meg's favorite." Rachel ran her fingers through her frizzy hair.

"Let's play a trick on Meg and Thomas," Courtney said suddenly. "See if we can separate them." Her eyes gleamed through her glasses. "Let's tell her Jordan got lost and Thomas went back to find her. Send her off on the wrong trail."

"That would teach her." Rachel danced up and down. "We should do it."

Cam shook her blonde head. "It will hold us up. We've got to get to the stone horse and back to camp before dark."

"We've got lots of time," Courtney snapped back. "It's not even three o'clock yet."

"Make up your mind," warned Dee-Dee. "Here comes Meg."

"All right." Cam nodded quickly as Meg approached, leading Cody.

"Where's Thomas?" she asked, as if on cue.

Rachel looked off in the distance. "Well, guess what, big surprise. Jordan, your little pet, got lost. And Thomas, your big pet, went to look for her."

Meg gulped back her annoyance. "Which way did he go?"

Rachel pointed in the wrong direction. "Sort of ... that way. Wouldn't you say, girls?"

The others nodded.

"All right," Meg said briskly. "Let Jesse know I've gone to find them. Start without us and we'll catch up. Thomas knows the way."

She climbed on Cody's back and headed in the direction they'd pointed—away from the stream and off trail.

CHAPTER 14

MUD SLIDE

At the same time, Rocco was getting a mini-lesson in manners. "Don't let him butt you with his head like that when you're working with his cinch," Thomas told Jordan. "In horse language, he's being rude."

"Anybody can pick on me—even a horse," Jordan said sadly. "I used to wish I had a horse more than anything. But maybe I'm the wrong kind of person to have one. I'm not tough."

"You're tough enough," Thomas assured her. "Put your hand up, like this. Block his move. It's not strength that does it, it's determination."

"But he's so strong ..." Jordan bit her lip. "If he wants to do something like head-butt me, how can I stop him?"

"Do what I showed you—you'll see."

Jordan grasped the cinch, and when Rocco turned his head into her, she thrust her hand up in his face.

"That's better! See? He swings his head away when he knows you mean business."

"I guess it's a start." Jordan looked happier.

"One step at a time. You'll do it," promised Thomas. "But right now we should get back to Meg and the others. They must be ready to go."

"Where's Meg?" he called as they neared the group.

"Didn't she find you?" Dee-Dee's eyes were wide with innocence.

"She went to look for you," Rachel said. "Ten minutes ago."

"That way ..." Courtney pointed vaguely up the mountain.

"Why would she go off in that direction?" Thomas looked puzzled. "We were just over there by the stream." He sprang onto Palouse's back in one amazing leap that left the four girls gasping. "I'll go get her."

Jordan looked at their hostile faces. "Thomas?" she pleaded. "Can I come?"

"Sure."

Jordan scrambled onto Rocco's back and urged him after Palouse. This time, he seemed to understand that she really meant business. Instead of balking or weaving off sideways, he followed Palouse politely, with Jordan, beaming, on his back.

"Should we wait for them?" asked Becky, glancing at her watch.

"We'll start slowly." Jesse positioned Tailor at the front of the group. "With any luck they'll catch up to us soon. If they don't, we'll stop and wait."

They set off, with Alison behind Jesse, Becky at the end of the string, and the campers in the middle.

Twenty minutes later, as the trail narrowed and ran along the bottom of a cliff, the four campers carried on a hushed conversation. There was still no sign of Thomas, Meg and Jordan.

"That didn't turn out exactly as we planned," Dee-Dee muttered back to Rachel. "Now Jordan and Meg have Thomas all to themselves!"

"I don't know what they both see in that Jordan," grumbled Courtney. "Why did Thomas take her with him?"

"If we're asking why," Cam sighed, "why did we play that stupid trick in the first place?"

"What's that noise?" Rachel suddenly pulled Shane to a stop.

A rumbling filled the air. It sounded like a freight train roaring past on the mountainside above them.

They looked up. Now the sound seemed to be coming from all around. The earth shook under their feet.

"RIDE!" screamed Becky behind them. "It's a mud slide!"

Ahead, Alison and Jesse were spurring their horses up the trail, leaning forward. The four campers followed, howling with fear.

"Oh no!"

"I don't want to die."

"Run, you stupid horse ..."

"GO! GO! GO!"

The rumbling turned to thunder. Trees snapped with a sound like pistol shots. Above the riders, a wall of rocks and mud tore down the slope, picking up more tree roots and stones as it came.

Becky could see it was heading straight at them. There was no escape except speed. Shadow knew. The mustang's nostrils flared as she gulped for air and raced along the narrow trail.

Ahead, Becky saw Alison and Jesse clear the leading edge of mud. The four campers were almost through. Jesse was off his horse, helping them.

Becky could smell the mud—a rank, earthy smell like a freshly dug hole. Close, almost on her. She glanced up and then away in terror. The wall of mud was as high as a house. It would bury her without a trace.

"Go, Shadow!" she screamed, and felt the horse dig deep for one last burst of effort.

The mud caught at her back hooves. Shadow screamed a horse scream of fear and defiance and kicked free.

The mud thundered past, snapping and cracking trees like matchsticks below. Becky lowered her head to Shadow's silvery mane and gulped with relief. When she looked up, she could see in the frightened faces of the others what a close call she'd had.

Shaking, she slid from Shadow's back. "Thanks," she whispered to the mare. "Good job."

Then Alison's arm was around her shoulders.

"I was so scared! I thought you were ... going to get buried in the mud."

"I'm all right, thanks to Shadow." Becky was still shaking. She couldn't bear to look at the devastation behind her. She only prayed that, somehow, Meg, Thomas and Jordan had escaped.

She didn't notice that Jesse had collapsed on the ground gripping his left leg.

CHAPTER 15

Split Group

Meg, Thomas and Jordan threw themselves to the ground while the earth shook beneath them. The horses whinnied in terror.

When the roaring in her ears died down, Meg took a harsh breath. Thomas had one arm across her shoulders and another across Jordan, protecting them.

"Wh-what happened?" Jordan whispered.

Thomas sat up with a glance at Meg. "You okay?" he asked softly.

"Mmm." Meg wanted his arm around her again.

Jordan wriggled to a sitting position. "Was it an earthquake?"

Thomas shook his head and pointed down the mountain. "A mud slide. The whole mountainside is saturated with water from the rain. It just slid away."

Meg looked in horror where he was pointing. There was no trace of the trail—only a smooth slope of raw mud. "What about the others?" she gasped. "They were right in the path of the slide!" She couldn't catch her breath. "What if ...?" she cried as if in pain. If Becky, Alison and the others were under the mud, there would be no way to save them. They would be buried alive.

"Where are they?" Jordan started to cry. Tears made channels down her dirty cheeks.

Thomas was searching the slide with his keen eyes. Above it was a dish-shaped shallow crater. Below, the gray mud fanned out like icing melting down a cake. Farther still, a tangle of broken trees, rock and debris formed a sort of dam.

At the junction of the mud and the wall of debris he saw movement.

"Look!" Thomas grabbed Meg's arm and pulled her to her feet. "Down there." He pointed.

At first Meg couldn't see anything but mud and destruction. Then her eye caught a flash of purple. She turned to Thomas. "I can see Alison in her purple jacket."

Thomas was counting. "Five, six, seven. They're all there. They look okay."

Meg slumped back to the ground. The weight of fear had lifted, but now she was limp with relief. She gazed up at Thomas. "They must be worried about us—can you signal them that we're all right?"

"I'll try." Thomas stared down the expanse of gray mud. "If I can get their attention."

"Maybe if we all shout," suggested Jordan, wiping her eyes with her sleeve.

They shouted and screamed at the top of their lungs. Meg and Jordan jumped in the air and waved their arms. Thomas picked up a tree branch and waved it in a large arc over his head.

"I can't hear what they're shouting," Becky called over her shoulder to Alison. "But I see the three of them above the slide. They're okay!"

"I wish *we* were," Alison muttered. "You'd better come over here."

She was kneeling by Jesse's side. He was holding his left leg, grimacing in pain. Beads of sweat trickled down his gray face.

"... Pulled my hamstring," he groaned. "Slipped on the mud."

"Jesse was trying to lead my horse away from the slide," Dee-Dee cried. Her face was scrunched up with concern. "Cloudy got scared and wouldn't go."

"He saved us all," Rachel squealed hysterically. "If it wasn't for Jesse, we'd be six feet under! Us, and the horses, and everything."

Cam stroked Spencer's quivering neck. "How can we get to the top now?" she asked in a shaky voice.

"We can't," Becky gulped. "The slide has blocked the path."

Alison gave Cam a hard look. "Anyway, we have to get Jesse some help before we do anything else."

"I guess we can forget about our trophy …" Cam said in a low, defeated voice.

"That's right," said Becky firmly. As if a dumb trophy was important right now!

Somebody has to take charge, she thought desperately. Jesse's hurting, and Alison can't think of anything but looking after him. The campers seemed stunned by their close call with the mud. Cam was as pale as a ghost, Rachel hysterical, Courtney too traumatized to say anything, and Dee-Dee shaking like a leaf.

Becky felt the trembling in her own legs. She looked at her watch. Three-thirty. With a detour around the slide, they'd be lucky to get back to Burnt Creek Camp, let alone the ranch, before dark.

A glance at the sky told her this wasn't their only problem. Thunderclouds were piling up against the peaks to the west. They could be in for a storm. Rain could trigger more mud slides.

Becky wished she had Meg's steady presence to help her make decisions right now. How had they ever got separated? she wondered. Trying frantically to remember her first aid rules, she stumbled over to Jesse and squatted beside him. "We should get your leg higher than your head while we decide what to do," she gasped. "If we had ice …"

Jesse tried to grin. "Forget the ice. The only question is, how can I ride?"

"Are you crazy?" Alison began rolling spare raincoats to prop up Jesse's leg. "Look at you—you're gray as those storm clouds up there, and sweating! Maybe you have internal injuries."

"My leg's not broken." Jesse's grimace of pain twisted his face. "Nothin' serious—just a torn ligament."

Alison shook her finger at him. "You always say that! Remember when you broke your wrist on our first trip? You kept pretending you were all right until you almost fell off your horse. Don't do that again."

"I didn't get much sympathy from you that time, as I remember," Jesse teased. "At least, not till we got chased up a tree by that grizzly."

"Well, I didn't know you then," Alison sniffed. "Now I know you wouldn't complain unless you were dying. You're not—are you?"

"He'll be fine," Becky promised her. She'd lived on ranches where cowhands worked hard and injuries were common.

She knew Jesse's wasn't life-threatening, but she'd seen her dad with a torn hamstring and knew it was a bad pain that didn't go away fast. The real danger was that he could go into shock.

"Rest awhile," Becky suggested. "Then, if we help you on Tailor and go slowly, you might be able to ride." She pulled Alison to her feet. "Come on, Nurse Alison. Quit sniffling and go find some dry wood. Girls!" she hollered to the campers. "We're going to get a fire started and heat some water."

They needed a hot drink before they got back on their horses, or there would be more accidents.

The campers scrambled to obey. There were no more cracks about Bossy Becky or grumbling about work. With worried glances at Jesse, they hurried to find firewood.

"I sure wish you'd never thought of that stupid trick we played on Meg," Dee-Dee whispered to Courtney.

"Don't rub it in," Courtney moaned. "I'm feeling bad enough already."

Thomas pointed to the summit of Mustang Mountain. It was wreathed in dark clouds. Seen from here, the stone horse looked like a jumble of massive stone shelves piled on one another. "Our only way back is over the mountain," he told Meg and Jordan.

"Couldn't we go down around the slide and meet up with the others?" Meg asked. She had no desire to ride higher. It was already after four, and it looked like rain again.

"There's no safe trail for the horses," Thomas explained. "The slide cut off the route we climbed, and any other is way too steep."

He patted Meg's shoulder. "Don't worry. We'll camp near the top and go down the other side of the mountain to the ranch tomorrow."

"You talk as if this whole place was your back-yard," sighed Meg, waving her arms to take in the vast panorama of mountain peaks and valleys surrounding them. "As if you could just fly over it like an eagle or run through it like a wild horse."

Thomas nodded. "That's how I feel," he said. "And that's how you'll feel when you come to live here. It's strange to you now, because you come from the city. But you belong here, Meg, just as I and the horses and eagles do. You know that." He reached for her hand.

"A-hem!" Jordan broke in. "Shouldn't we get going? Rocco's restless with all this standing around."

Meg realized she'd forgotten about Jordan for a minute. Looking into Thomas's dark brown eyes always had that effect on her.

She tossed back her ponytail and smiled at Jordan. "Yes, we should. Do you want to ride Cody for a while?"

"No." Jordan shook her head. "Rocco's going better for me now. Thomas showed me a few things."

"If you're sure ..." Meg looked doubtfully at the younger girl. "It's not going to be easy from here on. It looks like a pretty steep climb to the top."

"I'll lead, and you ride behind, on Cody," Thomas suggested. "Jordan's doing fine." His smile took them both in.

"All right," sighed Meg. She hadn't seen any great improvement in Jordan's riding since she and Thomas had joined her, but there was no way to talk her out of it.

Jordan's face was set with determination as she climbed on Rocco's back.

What were those girls thinking of—sending me on the wrong trail to look for Thomas and Jordan! Meg thought angrily. Were they just jealous because Jordan was getting some attention? Whatever the reason, it was a disaster. They were now separated for the rest of the trip.

They set out, leaning forward to help their horses up the slope. Soon they reached the tree line. Above that, nothing grew except moss and lichens and tufts of tough grass. Everything was gray—the stones under their horses' hooves, the rocky peak above them and the sky.

Meg was astonished when she saw a stud pile beside the slender trail.

"Thomas!" she called forward to him. "Wild horses? Up here?"

"Whose track do you think we're following?" he called back. "They must have a route over the mountain. Let's hope there's a sheltered place near the top on the other side where we can spend the night."

Meg nodded but she was thinking, spend the night? Our blankets, our tents and our food are all back at Burnt Creek Camp. All we have are emergency supplies.

CHAPTER 16
DRAGGED!

Several hours later, Thomas, Meg and Jordan were still climbing the wild horse trail to the top. It led them over stony ridges and through narrow gaps between the rocks. Rocco and Cody stumbled often. Their hides were caked with salt from sweating. Palouse was tireless, but Meg saw that the two other horses were exhausted.

"Maybe we should stop and rest the horses," Meg called.

Thomas swung around in the saddle. "We can stop if we need to," he shouted back, "but the summit is just ahead."

"Let's keep going," Jordan spoke up. "I'm not tired. Do you think we'll see the wild horses? I hope so!"

She was trying to impress Thomas, Meg thought. His

kindness had made Jordan's eyes brighten. She could re-member how, two years ago, Thomas had boosted her confidence with horses—how he made her feel that she could do anything—even tame a wild horse with her bare hands. He was doing the same for Jordan.

Another half hour of steady climbing brought them to the summit. From here, an amazing vista spread before them. Range upon range of snowcapped peaks marched away to the west, where the sun was setting. A cool wind blew in their faces, and the rain clouds seemed close enough to touch. It had started to drizzle.

"We made it!" Jordan looked around excitedly. "The very top of Mustang Mountain. Where's the cave in the stone horse's nose?"

"It's behind that rock bluff." Thomas turned Palouse and rode back to show her. "It's a deep hollow under a sharp overhang of rock."

"Do you really think there's jade in the cave?" Jordan squinted her eyes to look at him.

"No," said Thomas, "I don't. Most of the jade deposits are farther west."

"Can't we at least go look?" Jordan begged. "We're so close to the cave. If I could get the trophy for our cabin ..." She bit her lip. "Maybe those guys would stop treating me like the world's biggest loser!"

"Do you think we should, Meg?" asked Thomas.

"Not now." Meg urged Cody forward. "We've got to find a place to get out of the rain—some shelter for the night."

"We could sleep in the cave!" Jordan cried hopefully.

"There's no place for the horses," said Thomas, "and no water. Sorry."

Jordan looked back longingly toward the stone horse as they rode on. Meg could see her disappointment in the slump of her shoulders.

A very steep switchback trail zigzagged down from the peak. "Don't look down," Meg called to Jordan as it switched right, then left, then right again. "Keep your eyes on the trail ahead."

Jordan didn't answer. She was biting her lip too hard to speak. At one point, Thomas and Palouse were directly below her, and Meg and Cody right above. Rocco didn't like the sharp turns. He stopped, planted his feet and refused to move.

"Rocco—go!" Jordan pummeled him with her heels.

Meg shouted down to her, "You'll have to get off and lead him to the bottom of this steepest part."

"Stubborn horse!" Jordan climbed off Rocco's back and took a grip on his lead rope.

"Hold it closer to his head—" Meg started to yell, but it was too late. Instead of letting Jordan lead him around the switchbacks, Rocco took off down the almost vertical slope, dragging Jordan behind him. Her feet flew out from beneath her. She careened down the muddy mountainside on her back, shrieking.

"Help!"

Meg held her breath. Jordan could break her neck being bounced over rocks like that! She kicked Cody into a fast shuffle around the bends of the trail.

Thomas spurred Palouse at an angle to catch the runaway Rocco in his headlong flight down the mountain. Bending low to grab Rocco's reins, he pulled him to a halt.

Jordan slid to a stop at Palouse's feet. She pulled off her helmet and swiped the mud from her face. "I don't know what happened!" she cried furiously. "I was supposed to be leading Rocco, but he just took off!"

"Are you all right?" Meg had reached them. She leaped off Cody and ran to Jordan.

"I'm fine!" Jordan sat up. "I just can't understand that horse—why did he run ahead?"

She doesn't seem to be hurt, Meg thought with relief. Just a bit shaken—and very mad at Rocco.

Thomas was trying to calm the excited horse. "Next time," he instructed Jordan, "hold the lead rope closer to Rocco's head. Don't give him so much room to get away. And if he does, let go of the rope."

"There's not going to be a next time!" Meg announced. "Jordan, you ride Cody from now on. And don't give me an argument." She looked from Jordan's smudged and angry face to Thomas's doubtful one. "This isn't exactly the time for a riding lesson."

"I thought you were my friend." Jordan glared at her. "You won't let me get a trophy from the cave or ride Rocco. I want to show Rachel and the others, but you won't help me." She threw Thomas a despairing glance. "Why do you let her boss us around like this?"

"Uh—you'll have another chance to ride Rocco,"

Thomas promised. "Right now, you'll be safer on Cody."

Meg knew he wanted to reward Jordan's courage by letting her get back on Rocco. His face was blank as he helped her into Cody's saddle and adjusted the stirrups. Meg had seen that blank look before. It meant Thomas disagreed but wasn't going to say anything.

As she lengthened Rocco's stirrups, Meg felt like a bossy big sister. She was the bad guy, the enforcer. How did I get in *this* position? she wondered.

Below the switchback, the trail soon entered a small grove of stunted pines. A rock outcrop above them sheltered them from the worst of the wind and weather. A trickle of water down its face provided the horses with a welcome drink.

Meg sighed with relief as she slid from her saddle. Her legs almost buckled with weariness. At least the drizzle had stopped.

Thomas walked over to her, carrying a wool blanket. "I always carry an emergency cover," he said, looking down at her with warmth in his brown eyes. "You and Jordan can share it and wrap up in the rain slickers tonight. I'll get a fire going."

"Thomas ..." Meg sighed. "I don't mean to be bossy. But we've already got separated from the group, survived a mud slide and watched Jordan get dragged down a mountain. This trip is a disaster. We don't need anything else to happen!"

Thomas nodded and handed her the blanket. "I'll get some wood," was all he said.

Meg swallowed hard, thinking that if Jordan wasn't with them, she and Thomas might be the ones sharing that blanket! Why was she always trying to get close to him, and why was he always trying to move away?

A long way down the other side of the mountain, Alison, Becky, Jesse and the campers were faced with a wall of tangled trees, rocks and mud that marked the end of the mud slide.

At seven-thirty, the shadows were lengthening and the air growing cooler.

"We'll never get past this mud dam," Alison groaned. "It totally blocks our trail."

"But if we don't get back to Burnt Creek, we'll have no food," wailed Rachel.

"Or sleeping bags," moaned Cam.

"Or tents," added Dee-Dee.

"We'll have to sleep on the ground," Courtney snuffled, "like dogs."

"What do you think?" Becky turned to Jesse. He had ridden this far with clenched teeth and a white face. His left leg stuck out at an awkward angle.

Jesse shifted uncomfortably in the saddle. "Well, much as I'd like to get off this horse, I say we keep going and try to get around this heap of stuff. We still have some hours of daylight left."

CHAPTER 17

UP TO THE CAVE

"We're not going to make Burnt Creek Camp tonight," Becky announced two hours later. "This brush is too thick and there's no trail. We'll have to camp right here."

Four girls gaped at her.

"Here? It's not exactly the Rocky Mountain Hilton," Courtney protested.

"But there's water for the horses." Becky pointed to a small stream.

"Which means we'll be sleeping in a swamp!" Rachel's voice rose.

"Who cares where we sleep if we're not going to get the trophy?" Cam muttered. Since the mud slide, she'd sunk into gloom.

"Forget your dumb trophy!" Dee-Dee turned on her.

"We're lost in the wilderness with nothing but three chocolate bars and cheese and crackers."

"You've got chocolate bars?" The other three campers converged on Dee-Dee's saddlebag.

"GIRLS!" Alison shouted. "Lay off. Our food has to last till we get back to the camp. We can't go any farther because Jesse's in pain, and this is the best camping place we're likely to find before dark. So quit whining and try to make the best of it."

Becky grinned. Three years ago, her city cousin Alison would have been the one to complain the loudest. Even though she sometimes slipped back to her spoiled, self-centered ways, three summers on Mustang Mountain had changed her a lot. "First thing you have to do is unsaddle your horses and bring them over here," she told the tired girls. "I'm going to put up a picket line we can tie them to."

"How will we keep warm if we sleep here?" Dee-Dee quavered.

"We can use the saddle pads as blankets—no, don't complain that they smell like horse sweat—they're better than nothing." Becky took a coiled rope from her saddle and started to set up a line between two trees where she could tie the horses.

Alison was helping Jesse off Tailor. He had to dismount on the wrong side, and Alison held Tailor's head so he wouldn't make any sudden moves. "Almost there," she told Jesse as he lowered his body painfully to the ground. "I'm sorry. That's got to hurt." She hurried to unsaddle Tailor.

"Let's get a fire going before we lose the light," Jesse grunted as he hopped away from Tailor. "The wolves might be out again tonight."

While Becky and the campers hurried to find dry wood and build a fire, Alison stayed with Jesse and tried to make him comfortable. She propped his leg on his saddle to ease the pain and folded her jacket to make a pillow under his head.

"Who would have thought we'd ever be together again like this?" she whispered.

Jesse gave a muffled grunt.

"I mean, I know you're in too much pain to appreciate the amazing coincidence," Alison said. "But do you realize it's almost exactly three years since our first ride together?"

Jesse grunted again.

"It was a blizzard, that June," Alison sighed. "Remember? We were up to our armpits in wet snow. And you were hurt, just like now."

She got up to get a bottle of water, then sat by him again.

"Do you think it's our destiny?"

"I hope not!" Jesse rolled painfully on his side. "I can think of better destinies than to get busted up and sleep out in the cold every time I see you."

"I didn't mean that!" Alison gulped. "I meant, don't you think we sort of belong together?"

"Ohhh." Jesse let out a long groan.

"What's the matter?"

"Alison, I'm way too old for you." He reached up and patted her short dark hair. "I like you a lot, you're a great kid, but ..." He let his hand slide off her head. "I wish you wouldn't talk like this."

"Okay," Alison sighed. "I know you're hurting and cold. Let me get you a warm drink." She rose from her knees, trying not to feel the sting of his words. What was six years? Lots of people had older boyfriends and girl-friends! Even Chuck was older than she was.

At the memory of Chuck, Alison felt a twinge of guilt. He had been so totally out of her mind since she left the ranch—it was as if he didn't exist. She glanced back at Jesse, and all thoughts of Chuck disappeared. Jesse had pulled his hat over his face. He was even more adorable lying down and helpless than standing up!

As darkness fell on the other side of Mustang Mountain, near the peak, Thomas, Meg and Jordan made camp for the night. Thomas gathered as much dead wood as he could find, but none of the living trees. "These pines might be hundreds of years old, even though they're so scrawny," he told Meg, running his hand over the spiky green needles. "They've fought for life in poor soil and bad weather. The wind has shaped and twisted them like old men after a hard life."

"Don't worry. We'll be warm enough." Meg smiled at him. She loved the way Thomas talked. He respected everything that lived, from trees to horses.

They huddled near their small fire as the sky darkened from purple to black.

"Jordan's already asleep," Thomas said softly, pointing to the small snoring lump in the makeshift bedroll.

"She's a brave kid." Meg grinned in the dark. "She's still mad at me, but she didn't complain about freeze-dried peanuts and raisins for dinner." She looked at Thomas's profile, glowing in the firelight. "Maybe we should try to get some sleep, too."

"I'm going to sit up for a while," Thomas said. "But you should rest."

"I'll stay awake with you," Meg murmured.

"If you like." Thomas put his hand over hers and she felt its warmth all the way up her arm. "But let's not talk. I think the wild horses are out there, and I want to listen for them."

Meg sighed and leaned close to him. This is what all their dates would be like, she thought. In the future she could see herself trekking with Thomas all over the northern wilderness, following caribou herds, tracking horses, and cougars and bears ...

Before she knew it, her eyes had closed and she had fallen asleep leaning against Thomas's shoulder.

He gently lowered her to the ground beside Jordan and covered her with half the blanket and her yellow slicker.

The far-off howl of a wolf rose into the night. Thomas built up the fire till it blazed brightly, then stole away into the darkness.

Meg woke hours later to a chorus of wolf howls.

She sat straight up, shivering in the cold.

"Thomas ..." she called softly.

There was no answer, only another howl from farther down the mountain.

Meg patted the bedroll beside her. "Jordan, wake up!" But the bedroll was empty. Jordan was gone, too.

Meg was alone beside the dying fire.

She threw the blanket aside and reached for her flashlight. Where had those two gone?

All at once she remembered Jordan's passion to explore the cave at the stone horse. Could she have climbed up to it in the darkness? Had Thomas gone with her?

Meg fumbled furiously for the flashlight in her pack. She wasn't staying by herself in the middle of a pack of howling wolves. How dare they go without her?

She switched on her light. Clouds covered the moon—it would be pitch dark climbing to the top of Mustang Mountain.

Meg could hear the horses rustling around in the trees where Thomas had picketed them. Were they safe from the wolves? She went to check. Cody and Rocco were tied to a picket line between two stunted trees. Palouse was gone.

Shivering, Meg stroked Cody's dark mane. "Did they both ride Palouse up the mountain?" she asked aloud. She wanted to throw her leg over Cody's bare back and ride after them, but that would mean leaving Rocco alone, with the wolf pack circling. The two horses were safer together.

Shining her flashlight on the upward trail, Meg struggled up the steep switchback, the light bouncing as she climbed.

Halfway up, its narrow beam caught a heap of fresh horse manure just as she was about to step in it.

"A stud pile!" Meg breathed in astonishment. "The wild horses came this way just a little while ago."

She studied the hoofprints on the trail.

They were headed down the mountain.

Perched there on the dark trail, Meg flashed back to the first time she'd seen wild horses. That was when Thomas's wild stallion, a beautiful flame-colored horse called Wildfire, galloped off with the Mustang Mountain Ranch mares. Then there was the herd of wild horses she'd watched flying across a wide-open Wyoming plain. Her own horse, Patch, was one of those Wyoming mustangs, adopted from the wild. They were some of the most magical creatures alive.

This wild stallion had added to his stud pile recently. It hadn't been there when they rode down—Thomas would have seen it. Now the horses must be below their camp, somewhere in the trees.

No wonder the wolves were gathering.

Meg sprinted up the twisting trail, panting with the effort. She must hurry!

At the top, she shone her light around the tumbled

rocks that formed the stone horse. Huge blocks of stone loomed above her. Where was the cave?

She listened hard and heard noises coming from the left. Around the outcrop. That's what Thomas had said.

"Thomas!" she cried. "Thomas, are you there?"

"Meg! Help me!"

It was Jordan.

Meg edged around the outcrop of rock, careful not to look down at the abyss to her left. Below the stone horse, the mountain fell away in a swooping col, like a shallow bowl.

The cave was right in front of her. Her flashlight penetrated the darkness and showed Jordan at the very back, where the ceiling was low. She was crouched on the ground, holding on to something. Thomas? Was he hurt?

Meg stooped low and rushed into the cave's cold dampness, where her flashlight revealed Jordan with her arms around—a huge rock.

"I'm so glad you're here," Jordan cried. "I found the jade, but it's too heavy for me to lift."

Meg shone the light on the pale green boulder Jordan was hugging.

"Isn't it beautiful?" Jordan got to her knees and tried to move the rock. "Unnh! I just can't budge it."

"Of course you can't. You're crazy coming up here in the middle of the night. Where's Thomas?" The words burst from Meg.

"Thomas?" Jordan looked up. "I don't know. He was gone when I left. Stop shining that light in my eyes."

"You mean you came alone?" Meg sagged to the ground beside her, letting the light drop. "Why?"

"Because I want to be the one who brings back the trophy. Then those girls will have to stop calling me a loser." Jordan's voice was defiant.

"I understand." Meg reached out and touched the cold stone. "But you can't bring this back. Even if it is pure jade, we can't carry it."

"But it's so perfect! We could roll it down."

"Jordan!" Meg took Jordan's narrow face between her hands. "Listen to me. You can't roll a rock this big down a mountain. It could start an avalanche. It could hurt someone."

At that moment, a wolf howl rose eerily from the slopes below. Another joined in, and then another.

Meg picked up her light. "We have to get back!" Her voice crackled with urgency. "Thomas is out there. The wolves must be hunting the wild horses. C'mon."

"I'm staying here." Jordan shook her head stubbornly. "I'm not leaving my trophy."

Then stay! Meg wanted to shout at her, but she gulped back the words.

"Come with me now and I promise we'll ask Thomas to help you get the rock back to the ranch."

"You're just trying to get me out of here." Jordan threw her arms around the boulder again.

"Yes, I am," Meg admitted, "because I'm worried about Thomas and I think we should go and help him. But Jordan, Thomas is smarter than anybody I know. I know he'll try to find a way to get the trophy back."

"All right. For Thomas," Jordan said slowly. "If you promise promise *promise* to come back."

"I do. Let's go." Meg knew she couldn't keep the promise, but she had to get Jordan out of there. She seized her hand and they stooped and ran to the cave entrance.

Together they zigzagged down the switchback trail to their campsite. Still no Thomas, but here the howling of the wolves sounded much closer.

"What should we do?" Jordan's voice came out of the dark.

"We'll take the horses," Meg said breathlessly. "Try to find Thomas. We'll be safer on horseback."

She wedged her flashlight in a fork of a pine near Cody and Rocco. "Can you ride bareback?"

"I—I never have." Jordan's voice shook.

"Then we'd better take the time to saddle Cody." Meg reached for Cody's saddle. Jordan ran for his bridle, which Thomas had hung on another tree—this time, there was no argument about which horse Jordan should ride.

Fumbling, trying to hurry in the poor light, they managed to get the horse tacked up. Meg boosted Jordan onto Cody's back.

The wolves' howling rose higher and closer.

"Hurry!" Meg cried. "Follow me, and whatever you do, stay close."

CHAPTER 18

WOLF KILL

The howling echoed over the camp on the other side of the mountain.

"I can't sleep," Rachel moaned. "Those wolves ..."

"Even if there weren't any wolves, I couldn't sleep," grunted Courtney. "This saddle blanket doesn't cover my feet. My toes are freezing."

"And the ground is so hard!" Dee-Dee squeaked. "I've got a branch sticking into my back."

"So—move," groaned Cam. "And be quiet. Some of us are trying to sleep."

"I've *tried* that," Dee-Dee whined. "If I move, I roll downhill."

"If only those wolves would shut up!" Rachel sighed. "It sounds like they're trying to howl the place down!"

Listening to them grumble, Becky wondered why her mom and dad had ever dreamed this riding camp would work. Bringing five kids out here was insane! The wilderness is just too ... *wild* for them, Becky thought. The wolves weren't howling to annoy them. They were hunting for food to survive.

Becky tossed and turned on the hard earth, dreading what tomorrow would bring. They were a long way from the ranch. They couldn't travel fast with Jesse hurt. And if they weren't back by dinnertime tomorrow night, her mom and dad would have to notify the kids' parents they were lost. And that, Becky thought miserably, would be the end of that. No more camp. No more Mustang Mountain Ranch.

"Listen!" Rachel raised herself on one elbow. "The wolves have stopped howling."

Becky knew why. "The pack is closing in for the kill," she whispered. She hoped Meg, Jordan and Thomas were far from that hunt.

But Meg and Jordan were riding closer to the howling wolves. They entered another stand of lodgepole pines growing close together. In the dark, lit by flashlight beams, the trees looked like bars on a prison cell.

"Ahh-whooo!" came from their left.

"Ah-whooo!" from their right. The wolves were surrounding them.

The horses started and shied. Rocco tried to break from Meg's control. He wanted to panic and crash through the trees.

At that moment a hand shot out of the darkness and grabbed Rocco's halter.

"Get off your horse and turn off your light," Thomas said in a hushed voice. "The wild stallion's right over there. He thinks you're a threat and abandoned his mares and foals to face you. You too, Jordan. Get off and stand behind Cody. The stud won't be so threatened if he sees just horses."

Thomas's voice was husky with emotion. He was holding Palouse by the lead rope.

Meg instantly obeyed, slipping off Rocco's back and hiding behind him. Jordan did the same. "I can't see the stallion," she whispered.

"I don't want to shine a light on him, but he's close enough to see us clearly." Thomas edged the horses away. "He should be protecting his band from the wolves, but he thinks we're more dangerous."

Meg realized the howling had suddenly stopped. "The wolves have gone," she said.

"No," Thomas murmured, "they're preparing to attack."

The darkness of the thick forest felt like a blindfold. There was no sound except the breathing of their horses standing close to them.

But in the next moment, the darkness erupted in snapping and growling, whinnying and stamping.

Thomas turned on his light. "Stay here!" he ordered. In one leap he was on Palouse's bare back, riding away.

Meg shuddered at the sounds coming through the trees.

"What's happening?" Jordan cried.

"Get on Cody," Meg whispered. "No, wait!"

The terrible noises of the wolf attack had stopped.

Meg got on Rocco and rode forward, bending low over his neck, soothing him. He was quivering all over, snorting and unwilling to go. Meg thought she knew why. Horses hated and feared the smell of death.

As they moved slowly through the trees, Meg turned on her flashlight. In its beam she saw Thomas bending over the body of a fallen horse. He turned at the light and held his hand in front of his eyes.

"Don't come any closer," he told Meg. "And don't let Jordan come near."

"Did the wolves kill a horse?" Jordan's small voice rang out clearly. Her light snapped on.

"Yes," Thomas answered. "The stallion tried to drive off his mares, but this one had a young foal and she stayed to protect him. The wolves got her."

"What are we going to do?" Meg asked, her voice low and shaking.

"There's nothing we can do. As soon as we leave, the wolves will be back to feed. They're hungry. To them, the mare is a lifesaving meal. Many meals."

"Where is her foal?" Meg choked.

"I don't know. Maybe the wolves got him too."

"No, they didn't. Here he is!" Jordan had been searching the underbrush with her light. Now it shone on the dark coat of a young foal almost camouflaged by the bushes surrounding him. He looked confused by the light.

"He's too young to run." Meg jumped off Rocco. Jordan had already thrown her arm around the foal's neck and was stroking his spiky mane.

Thomas hurried over to them. "Just a few weeks old," he said, shaking his head. "Too young to survive without his mother."

"We could bottle-feed him!" Meg exclaimed.

"If we had a bottle, or milk." Thomas nodded. "If we're going to try to save him, we'll have to get him back to Mustang Mountain Ranch as fast as we can."

CHAPTER 19

CIRCLE OF SAFETY

Thomas gently laid the foal across Palouse's withers. The baby squirmed and wriggled and blinked in the bright light from Meg's flashlight.

"How long do we have?" Meg asked Thomas. "How long can he last without food?"

"It's hard to say." Thomas stroked the foal's fuzzy neck. "It depends when he last had a meal. But the sooner we get him back to the ranch, the better."

"Doesn't it hurt him, flopped over Palouse like that?" Jordan hovered around the foal like an anxious aunt.

"I've carried lots of foals this way," Thomas promised her. "He'll settle down once we get moving."

As they rode higher through the dense trees to their campsite, Thomas calculated how long it would take them to return to the ranch. "I figure about ten hours. Luckily it's not as long going this way as the Burnt Creek route."

"Jesse tried to pick an easy route for the campers," Meg explained.

"I can understand that," said Thomas, "but we'll make better time going down this side of the mountain, even carrying this little guy." He rubbed the foal's head between his small ears. "If we leave at first light and nothing goes wrong, we should be back at the ranch by late afternoon."

Meg was trying to picture their return. "I'm sure the ranch has baby bottles to feed a foal," she murmured. "Becky's mom will know what to do."

They reached their shelter under the stunted pines. Jordan leaped off Cody and ran to help Thomas gently lift the foal from Palouse's withers and set him on his tottery legs.

"He needs a name," Thomas said.

Jordan stroked his face. "A name? What color do you think he'll be?"

"Maybe blue roan, like his mother," Thomas told her.

"Oh!" Jordan gulped.

All three of them were suddenly silent, thinking of the foal's mother lying in the woods, and the wolves, gathering around her body.

Meg shuddered. "We can name him in the morning. Let's build up the fire and try to snatch some sleep before sunrise. Jordan—you look after him while we stoke the fire."

Only a few minutes later the horses were picketed, the fire glowing and Jordan sleeping with her arms around the foal's neck.

Meg and Thomas were alone—almost! Meg had a chance to tell Thomas about their adventure at the stone horse's cave.

"I promised Jordan we'd go back and show you her prize rock." Meg sank beside him by the fire. "But how can we? You said we should leave as soon as it's light."

Thomas put his arm around her shoulders and gently kissed her forehead. "Jordan might forget all about that rock. She has something more important to think about now than some silly camp trophy."

Meg was quiet, wondering. Thomas hadn't seen the way Jordan was hugging that rock. She wished she wasn't so tired and worried. Thomas was holding her close, kissing her, at last—even if it was just a comforting kiss on the forehead. If she wasn't so sad and exhausted, she would have been thrilled. Instead, her eyelids drooped, her brain buzzed and the last thing she remembered was Thomas tucking the blanket around her.

He brought the horses in closer and tethered them by the fire. Meg, Jordan and the foal slept on the other side. Thomas built the fire up as high as he could and then drew a mental circle around them all to keep them safe. He stayed awake, keeping the fire burning, in case the wolves were gathering for another attack.

As dawn lightened the sky, Thomas stopped looking for yellow eyes in the trees and listening for soft footfalls outside the circle of fire. He let his head droop and his eyes close.

The next thing Thomas knew, there was a wet snuffling in his ear. "Palouse! What do you want?"

The fire had died and the coals were smoking.

Through the screen of white smoke, Thomas saw why Palouse had woken him. The thin figure of a girl, shivering in the cold dawn, stood watching him from the other side of the firepit.

"Jordan, what are you doing?" Thomas stretched and stood up in one motion.

"I know we—have to get going—for the foal," Jordan faltered. "B-But I want you to come with me up to the stone horse. I want to get my trophy. Did Meg tell you about the jade?"

Thomas nodded. "She told me. You know that it might just be a green rock—not jade. Like I said, most of the jade in these mountains is to the west."

"But there's a legend about the stone horse," Jordan said stubbornly. "Cam told us." She was shivering even harder, her arms clenched over her chest.

"What about the foal?" Thomas pointed to where the colt slept beside Meg. "We can't take him up to the stone horse."

"Meg's here—she'll look after him." Jordan's words

tumbled over each other. "It won't take long ..."

Thomas looked at his watch. It was just past five—he'd only slept a few minutes. "We'll ask Meg," he said.

"Don't wake her up! *Please!* She'll say no. Let's just go," Jordan cried softly.

Thomas glanced at Meg and the foal, sleeping peacefully.

"All right," he whispered. "But it will have to be a fast trip." He reached in his saddlebag for the small hammer that he always carried.

He leaned his forehead against Palouse's and talked in a soft, low voice. "Horse, you look after Meg and the foal while we're gone. We'll soon be on our way, down to green grass and good grazing for you."

He set off at a run up the steep switchback trail, with Jordan puffing at his heels. She didn't complain at the pace, but threw herself down, panting, when they reached the cave mouth.

"It's—in—there." She pointed.

Dawn light streamed in on the jagged green boulder. It seemed to be lit from within.

Thomas let his breath out. "Whew! Looks like you might have found something special."

He bent and crawled into the depths of the cave. With a quick blow of his rock hammer, he struck the surface of the pale green rock.

"Come over here," he called to Jordan. "See those little white cracks?"

"It looks like you made a feather on the rock with

your hammer." Excitement lit Jordan's face. "What does it mean?"

"It's the test for jade." Thomas beamed. "And the rock passed. Help me roll it to the entrance."

"It's really truly jade? Can we take it back to camp?" Jordan begged.

"Let's get it out of here first." Thomas threw his strong shoulder into the job of moving the stone. In his mind was the image of Meg sleeping and the hungry foal. They must not take too long at this.

Jordan lent her weight, huffing and puffing. Slowly the rock rolled over—once, twice, and then, with Thomas at the limit of his strength, one more time out the cave opening.

Jordan waited, holding her breath to see what would happen next.

"I had to get it out here where I could get a good swing at it," Thomas grunted. He raised his hammer over his head and brought it down with all his force on a point of the boulder. The hammer bounced off, leaving more feathery white cracks.

"Jade is the toughest rock in the world," Thomas told her. "You have to hit it just right. One more try."

The rock gleamed green in the sun. Thomas swung his hammer and struck the stone. A sharp, shoe-sized flake fractured off and flew through the air.

"I'll get it!" Jordan scrambled to the cliff and plucked up the flake just before it tumbled over the edge. Cradling it in her arms, she ran back to Thomas.

"Thank you." Her hazel eyes sparkled. "This is a perfect trophy. It's so beautiful. Wait till the other kids see it. Look, Thomas!"

"I'll take a good look later," he promised. "Right now, we should get out of here."

He stood on the narrow ledge outside the cave and looked up at the looming rocks of the stone horse. "I don't like the way this feels," he said. "The mud slides have changed the mountain—destabilized it."

He set off at a run, around the outcrop and down the switchback trail. Jordan slid, tumbled and hurtled down the tight turns after him, the jade clutched to her chest.

The foal was on his feet, waving his bottlebrush of a tail, when they got back. Palouse stood over him, as if on guard.

Meg sat up, rubbing her eyes sleepily. "Where have you two been?"

Jordan's smile stretched from ear to ear. She held out her hands to Meg. "I got it, I got the trophy! Thomas broke this piece off the big boulder with his special hammer—"

"Is it jade?" Meg interrupted. She took the fragment of rock from Jordan and turned it in her hands, seeing its deep green color.

"Pure jade—the kind prized by carvers in China for five thousand years." Thomas grinned. "They carve great stone horses out of jade."

"I ... didn't think you'd go to the cave," Meg faltered. "I thought you wanted to leave early."

Thomas looked at his watch. "It's still only six o'clock." He ruffled Jordan's fine hair. "*Some* people were up real early."

Meg handed the jade back to Jordan, got up and stretched. She was stiff from sleeping on the hard ground.

She whipped the elastic off her ponytail and smoothed it back as well as she could. "I don't know how you two did it," she yawned. "We were up almost all night."

"I just had to try." Jordan's eyes were wide and shining. "Wait till Rachel and the others see this!" She held her trophy up to the sun.

"Put it in your saddlebag," ordered Thomas. "We should saddle the horses and get moving. The foal needs food."

"So do we—even if it's just chocolate and energy bars."

"That's okay." Jordan grinned. "I don't need food, now that I have the trophy." She strode over to the heap of gear on the ground and buckled the piece of jade into Cody's saddlebag.

"You sure made *her* happy," Meg whispered to Thomas as they saddled the horses, munching breakfast while they worked.

"She's a good kid." Thomas crumpled his energy bar wrapper and stuffed it in Palouse's saddlebag. "Thanks for looking after the camp," he whispered in Palouse's ear. "Now you have to carry the little guy, and we have to go fast."

142

As Thomas laid the foal over his withers again, Palouse stamped and whinnied.

"Something's wrong." Thomas smoothed Palouse's mane. "He's trying to tell me. What is it, my friend?"

CHAPTER 20

WHAT'S WRONG?

On the other side of the mountain, Becky's eyes snapped open. "Something's wrong," she said out loud. A feeling of dread had swept through her, waking her from a sound sleep.

For a second she had no idea where she was. Then the whinny of a horse in her ear brought it all back. "That's my horse, Shadow," she groaned to herself. "I'm lying on the ground and it's cold. And I'm starving!"

Worst of all, four miserable campers, a wounded cowboy and her cousin Alison all depended on her to get them out of this mess. Becky groaned and rolled over. None of them was awake. Maybe she could go back to sleep, too.

But that sense of onrushing doom wouldn't let her.

Something awful was going to happen if they didn't get moving. What could be more awful than this? she wondered. She truly dreaded the moment when Rachel, Courtney, Dee-Dee and Cam remembered there was nothing for breakfast but another square of chocolate and a handful of raisins and peanuts!

Quickly, she pulled on her boots and went to wake Alison.

"We should get going," she whispered. "How's Jesse?"

Alison pulled herself up on one elbow to look at the sleeping cowboy. Two days' growth of beard smudged his jaw. Above it, his tanned face was gray. "He hardly slept because of the pain," she sighed.

"He's asleep now," Becky pointed out.

"That's because I gave him pain medication at three this morning." Alison showed her a pill bottle. "Mom always makes me carry this in case I get a migraine. Jesse didn't want to take them yesterday because he said he had to stay alert to ride, but I figured in the middle of the night ..." She shrugged. "He was so out of it, he took them without complaining."

"How long do they last?" Becky asked. Jesse was snoring peacefully.

"About four hours," Alison said. "I only take one, because they're strong, but I gave Jesse two because he's so big. Can't we let him sleep a little longer?"

Becky ran her fingers through her tangled hair, trying not to scream at her cousin. Couldn't she understand they had to hurry? "If you can wake him up, I really think you should," she said slowly and firmly. "I'll wake the girls. We've *got* to get going, *now*."

"All right, all right, don't get excited. Maybe you need one of these to calm you down," she joked, rattling the pill bottle at Becky.

"No thanks, I'll pass." Becky turned on her heel and marched off to wake the girls on the other side of the cold fire.

On her way, she glanced at the top of Mustang Mountain, where the morning sun blazed on the stone horse. His flying mane seemed to be on fire. Somewhere up there were Meg and Thomas and Jordan. She wondered how they'd spent the night and if they were already on their way down to the ranch.

"At least Meg has Thomas," she muttered. "That must be a relief!" She wished she had Rob here to help. On her endurance ride last summer, Rob had been her crew. He had always known what to do and might have an idea how to get these campers moving.

Becky strode to the four sleeping lumps. "Time to get up."

Soon, the campers were singing a chorus of complaints as Becky shared out small portions of their remaining food.

"One measly square of chocolate?" Dee-Dee scrunched up her elfin face. "That's all we get?"

"My stomach growled all night," sighed Courtney. "This is child abuse."

"I've never been so famished in my entire life!"

Rachel cried, gobbling her square of chocolate in one gulp.

"If you take small bites and make it last," Cam spoke up, "it makes you feel fuller."

"I *hate* the way you nibble everything," Rachel muttered. "If you don't finish that chocolate, I'm going to grab it from you."

"Stop that!" Becky insisted. "Listen up. We're in a tough spot. We've got to fight our way around this wall of debris from the mud slide. Jesse's hurt, so we have to rely on ourselves. Our emergency rations must last another day—maybe more. So this is the last time I want to hear the word 'food,' do you understand?"

"We might see berries …" Rachel said hopefully.

"Too early in the season for berries." Becky shook her head. "That's why the animals are so hungry. You heard the wolves howling last night, right?"

The four girls nodded miserably.

"So let's go," Becky finished her orders. "Keep together and watch out for one another. We're going to make it back to the ranch today."

She looked at their miserable faces—this wasn't getting through. Suddenly she could hear Rob's voice in her head and the advice he'd given her when things were tough in the endurance race. Think of their strengths—give them something to do besides sitting here moping.

"Rachel!" She shook Rachel's shoulder. "I'm putting you in charge of the food. It's all in my saddlebag. From now on, you decide who gets to eat what."

Rachel looked up, blinking. "Oh. Okay. I'm on it." She struggled to her feet. "I'll see what we've got left ..."

Becky had already moved on. "Courtney! Take this." She reached in her pocket and pulled out her compass. "I want you to ride in front and make sure we don't go in circles. We're going to have trouble getting through this brush without a trail."

"Sure." Courtney reached for her glasses. "Uh—I can do that."

Becky put Cam in charge of the horses. "I want you to watch for sore feet or any other signs of stress," she told Cam. "We can't get back to the ranch without these horses."

Cam gave her one of her rare smiles and nodded. "All right."

Dee-Dee's job was filling the water bottles and reminding the riders to drink at regular intervals. "Here—" Becky yanked a small container out of another pocket and thrust it at Dee-Dee, "water purification pills. We might need them before this day is over."

Dee-Dee jumped to her feet and grabbed the container. "Don't worry. I'll make sure everybody drinks, and nobody gets poisoned."

"All right." Becky marched back to Alison and Jesse, who was now awake. "Alison, your one and only job today is taking care of that cowboy. Keep him moving, even if you have to *tie* him on his horse."

"That was a good speech, Becky," Jesse mumbled as Alison and Becky helped him onto Tailor. "But you

know it's gonna be real tough to reach the ranch by tonight. Those kids are goin' to get an awful lot hungrier
before they get full."

While the two groups of riders made their way down
opposite sides of Mustang Mountain, the stone horse on
its peak shifted. Chunks of loose rock rattled down the
cliff at its feet.

Palouse was carrying the foal and Thomas. He broke
into a swift jog on the wild horse trail from the peak.

"Easy, fella!" Thomas reined him in. "What's your
hurry?" Palouse sensed that something was wrong, too,
Thomas thought, but what?

Meg rode up beside Thomas on Rocco. The gray horse
tossed his head nervously. "What's the matter with these
horses?" she panted. "Rocco is acting crazy."

"I'm not sure." Thomas reined in Palouse and leaped
from his back. The tall Appaloosa was perspiring heav-
ily. His ears were laid back and his tail clamped.

"Palouse is afraid." Thomas stepped away to study
his horse. "He's been acting like this since we set out
this morning."

Jordan caught up to them. "That jogging was fun!"
Her face was red with excitement. "Are we stopping
here?"

At that second, they all heard a thunder from the
mountain—a deep rumbling, rolling sound.

"Another mud slide?" Meg gasped.

They looked up. The top of Mustang Mountain was tipped at a strange angle.

"Look out!" Thomas shouted. "It's going to fall."

Palouse panicked and raced for the trees, tossing the foal sideways into Thomas's arms.

Rocco reared and tried to follow. Meg gripped his lead rope and held on with all her strength.

Jordan sat in Cody's saddle, staring with wide-open eyes. There was no time to run or hide or take shelter.

The ground shook under their feet. They watched in horror as the top of Mustang Mountain broke apart and fell out of sight.

"It's falling down the eastern side!" Meg clapped her hand to her mouth. "Becky and Alison and the others are over there!"

CHAPTER 21

THE STONE HORSE

Boulders from the stone horse hit the wall of debris from yesterday's mud slide and bounced over Becky's head. She lay with the others, huddled close to the wall with their arms over their heads.

When the rumbling stopped, Becky sat up slowly.

She stared up at Mustang Mountain. The peak that she'd seen from the ranch for three years was flat on top.

"He's gone ..." She took a deep breath.

"Who?" Alison frantically wriggled to her feet. "Who's gone?"

"The stone horse." Becky was shaking from their narrow escape. "Those rocks that flew over our heads just now were part of him." She pointed at the top of the mountain.

"You mean his nose and the cave, and everything's gone?" Cam gasped. "How could that happen?"

"The mud slide must have undermined the base of the horse," Becky explained, trying to keep her voice from trembling. "This wall of mud and rocks and tree trunks saved us."

"I'll never find out if the legend was true—if there really was jade in the cave," Cam mourned.

Becky shook her head. "How can you still be thinking about jade? We're lucky to be alive."

Jesse pulled himself up on the trunk of a slender poplar. "Lucky! You can say that again. Is everybody okay? How about the horses?"

"I'll check." Cam scrambled to her feet and headed into the trees. They had hit the ground and let their horses go when they heard the rumbling. There hadn't been time to tie them.

She was back a few minutes later, her face white. "They're gone."

"Gone!" gasped Alison. "What do you mean?"

"They've just disappeared," Cam said desperately. "There's no sign of them anywhere." She took a deep breath, looking from one shocked face to another, waiting for an avalanche of angry accusations. "I know—I'm a total failure. All I had to do was look after the horses and I couldn't even do that."

Rachel said with a sigh, "You're not a failure. Who'd guess the whole mountain was going to come crashing down?"

"That's right," Dee-Dee agreed, her small face sober. "The horses must have been totally terrified."

"I know *I* was," Courtney gasped. "I thought the world had come to an end!"

"They're right. It's not your fault, Cam." Jesse winced as he lowered himself back to the ground. "Horses know before people when something like a landslide is going to happen."

Cam's face cleared like the sky after a storm. "Is that true?"

Jesse nodded. "We'll have to go look for them. If it wasn't for this leg ..."

"We're in real trouble ... aren't we?" Becky was still shaking.

"Yes, m'am." Jesse tried to smile. "It's a long walk back to the ranch."

"You can't walk at all!" Alison exclaimed.

Becky looked around at the ruined forest, littered with boulders and broken trees. "It's going to be tough tracking the horses," she said. "Tough even finding our way with no trail."

"Leave me some food and firewood and hike out of here," Jesse said. "I'll just slow you down. When you find the horses, or get some help, come back for me."

"We can't do that!" Becky exclaimed.

"Got a better suggestion?" Alison demanded, her hands on her hips. "You should get going. I'll stay with Jesse."

At Mustang Mountain Ranch, Chuck and the campers stopped their riding lesson when they heard the mountain roar. They watched in amazement as the stone horse broke apart and tumbled down the mountain's western slope.

Laurie and Dan Sandersen came running from the house. "Oh, what a pity," Laurie cried. "I loved that stone horse. The kids always thought he looked like a mustang running free."

"Speaking of the kids," said Dan, "our bunch wouldn't be anywhere near there, would they?"

"Oh, no, I don't think so." Laurie shook her head. "Jesse gave me his route plan. They rode up to the stone horse yesterday. By this morning they'll be on their way back from Burnt Creek Camp on the other side of the mountain."

"I hope you're right," Dan muttered.

"Quit worrying." Laurie patted her husband's arm. "Becky and Jesse are sensible young adults. They'd never put the campers at risk. They'll be back tonight with all sorts of exciting stories."

Two weary hours later, Becky and the four campers had finally worked their way past the wall of debris but were still trudging through the thick forest of pines.

It was hard to see the sun overhead. Almost no light filtered through the dense dark green needles. No wind sighed through the branches, and the ground under their feet was soft and boggy, crisscrossed with moss-covered logs. With each footstep, they plunged into black muck.

It was bad terrain for horses, terrible for hikers. Becky was at home in the mountains on horseback. On foot, she felt weird. "We're lost," she told the others, sinking down on a log. "I haven't the foggiest idea which direction we're going."

"Southeast." Courtney pulled the compass out of her pocket. "And we're not going in circles, either. I've been checking."

"That's a relief." Becky brushed back her hair. "But we're moving at the speed of turtles."

"And we're almost out of food," Rachel added.

"And water," said Dee-Dee. She offered her hand to pull Becky up. "C'mon, let's keep moving. Maybe we can find a stream, or a spring, or something."

"I don't care if we ever get back," Cam said, her head in her hands. She had plunked down on a stump apart from the others.

"What do you mean?" Becky staggered to her feet and slogged over to Cam.

Cam raised her face. Her smooth features were a mask of despair. "I mean it. I don't care if we make it back to the ranch. I wanted to show my father that I could do something really hard. I thought bringing back a trophy from the stone horse would prove it. But now we're coming back with nothing—"

There was a silence for a moment, then Rachel let out a noisy sigh. "What's the matter? Does your father think you're a wimp or something?"

"Rachel!" Becky protested.

"No. Let her answer. I want to know." Rachel demanded, "Is that why you came to this camp—because you thought wilderness riding would be some kind of test to prove how tough you are? Well—look around—it is! We're tired and hot and lost without food or water or horses. If we make it out of here, it will be a miracle. Isn't that tough enough?"

"And anyway," Dee-Dee added, "why should you care what your father thinks? You know, and *we* know. All of us on this crazy out-trip. You've never quit. You've kept up. You're as tough as any of us."

Cam was staring at them with a confused look in her green eyes, like someone wrestling with a new idea.

They're right," Becky said quietly. "Nobody will ever really understand how brave you are, all of you. I'm as proud as if you were bringing back the biggest chunk of jade ever found."

Cam shook back her shoulders. "Maybe you're right." A tight smile turned up the corners of her mouth. "Who cares what my father thinks? Who cares what a big shot he is?"

"Just keep saying that," Rachel urged, "and you might even start to believe it."

"Let's keep walking." Becky started off, plodding through the boggy mud. "Anything's better than staying here. I'm beginning to hate the sight of pine trees."

They slogged on—Courtney in front with the compass, then Becky and the others.

Ten minutes later, Courtney tripped and fell. The compass flew out of her hand and disappeared in the mat of green moss. She stretched flat on the ground and was digging for it in the moss when something caught her eye. "Look." She pointed ahead. "What's that? Some kind of clearing?"

The others left her sprawled on the moss and dived for the glimpse of sunlight they could see through the trees.

"*Wow!*" Dee-Dee exclaimed in a hushed whisper. "What a beautiful sight!"

Just ahead, the forest ended in a strip of bare ground. "It's the clear-cut!" Becky cheered. "This will lead us right back to the ranch."

"We can see where we're going!" Cam's smile was suddenly wide.

"And walk a lot faster," said Rachel.

"We won't need to walk," Dee-Dee whispered again. "Look!"

Along the edge of the strip rode two men, leading a string of horses. They came closer.

Becky gasped, "The poachers—and they've got our horses!"

"What do you mean—poachers?" Rachel hissed.

"We thought they might be—never mind, I'll explain later." Becky remembered that the campers had never seen Bruce and his buddy. It didn't matter. Right now, she was determined to get their horses back, even if these two guys were ax murderers!

"Stop! Those are our horses," she shouted, running forward to intercept the riders.

The man on the paint horse gaped down at her in astonishment. "Where on earth did you girls come from?"

"Never mind. Our horses bolted when the top fell off Mustang Mountain." Becky pointed to the flat peak behind her. "We've been walking ... ever since ... looking for them. That's my paint, Shadow, the first in line. She's got a freeze brand from Wyoming ..."

"Okay." The man held up his hand. "I believe you. Bruce and I recognized these horses from the other day back at Burnt Creek. We wondered where you'd got to— figured you were in some kind of trouble."

"You did?" Becky gasped.

"Sure," the man called Bruce joined in. "We caught the horses streaming by our camp a couple of hours ago. Where's your friend, the tall cowboy?"

"Right back there." Becky pointed vaguely. She didn't want these men to know she and the girls were alone.

"Jesse wrenched his leg and we left him by the mud slide," Dee-Dee chimed in helpfully. "He couldn't walk at all."

"And the other counselor, Alison, stayed with him," Courtney added.

"She's his girlfriend," Cam volunteered.

"What kind of things do you poach?" Rachel went up close to Bruce. "Eggs? Fish? I would kill for a couple of poached eggs on toast right now."

Becky gulped. *Shut up, Rachel*, she wanted to shout, but it was too late. Bruce was staring at her.

"What on earth are you talking about?"

"Becky said you were poachers ..." Rachel frowned.

"Poachers!" Now the other man started laughing. He turned to Becky. "So you think Bruce and I are a pair of animal poachers? And I suppose you think we use these rifles to hunt illegally."

Bruce just sat on his horse, staring at Becky.

"It's none of our business. We just want our horses," Becky said bravely. Her knees were turning to water.

CHAPTER 22

CLEAR-CUT

"I think you better look at what we've got in these saddle-bags," Bruce said slowly. "You might find it interesting."

"No ... thanks." Becky's voice stuck in her throat.

"Just take a peek." Bruce leaned back and unbuckled his saddlebag. "I insist."

The other girls were suddenly silent, sensing Becky's fear. She took a hesitant step forward. What would she see? Grizzly hearts? Ram's horn? Worse?

Bruce reached into the bag and pulled something out.

A sudden gust of wind ruffled the thing in his hand, so Becky couldn't see clearly.

"Wha—what is it?" she stammered. He had something in a plastic sleeve. Something tiny—the size of a pencil eraser.

"What Bruce has is a DNA sample from a grizzly bear," the other man said. "We take samples to see which bears are related. That way, we can get an idea of a grizzly's breeding habits and the size of its range. We also use radio collars, and we shoot the animals with tranquilizers to attach them." He put his hand on the rifle hanging at his side.

"You shoot bears!" cried Dee-Dee behind her. "That's terrible."

"It doesn't hurt them," Bruce said. "It just puts them to sleep for a while."

"That's right." Now the other man was grinning. "We don't poach endangered species to sell. We study them. We're scientists."

"Oh!" Rachel rolled her eyes. "*That* kind of poacher! Sorry. My mind is stuck on food ... we're all kind of hungry."

"We can fix that." The first man hopped off his horse. "I'm Gord. I'm in charge of cooking on this trip. We'll get you fed and on your way."

Becky's head buzzed. She could hardly take it in. The strangers were good guys. The girls had got their horses back and would soon be full and on their way back to the ranch. It was almost too good to be true.

The foal lay limply over Palouse in front of the saddle. Its eyes were closed.

"How is our baby doing?" Meg rode up beside Thomas.

Thomas shook his head. "Not well. It's a long time since he's eaten. I don't know if he'll make it. We're still hours from the ranch."

"Should I tell Jordan?" Meg looked back at Jordan, riding Cody. She was riding much better than the day before. Kids learned fast, once they had some confidence.

"Not yet." Thomas shook his head. He stroked the foal's fluffy, soft coat. "Poor little guy. Maybe it would have been better to let him die with his mother last night than to put him through this. At least he would have died fast. I should know better than to interfere with nature."

"Don't say that!" Meg burst out. "The foal's mother gave her life to save him from the wolves. She told him to hide in the bushes, and he did. That counts for something."

"I guess so," muttered Thomas. "But I wish we had started as soon as I woke up. Getting Jordan's trophy cost us an hour, and that hour could be the difference between life and death for this foal."

Becky and the campers stuffed themselves with sandwiches and cookies from the scientists' saddlebags.

"Ooh, that's better," Rachel sighed, handing the

cookie bag to Courtney. The five of them were sitting on tree stumps along the edge of the clear-cut.

"Much better!" Courtney agreed, digging in the bag for the last cookie.

"I usually hate salami, but I ate three sandwiches." Cam laughed happily. "I feel like a new person!"

"I guess you don't mind so much about the trophy now?" Rachel glanced at her.

"No—" Cam's eyes widened in surprise. "You're right. I don't! We're not lost, and we're getting through this together. Nobody else is going to understand how amazing this trip has been ..." She suddenly looked as if another big load had been lifted. "... and *that* doesn't matter, either. We don't need a trophy. *We* understand."

She looks like a new person, Becky thought, gazing at Cam. Like she's dropped a huge weight she was carrying.

Becky bunched up her wax paper and carried it over to buckle in Shadow's saddlebag. "If you can spare any more food," she said to Bruce, "we should take some to Alison and Jesse. They must be starving."

"We've got lots of food, but why don't you let us deliver it, along with their horses." Bruce pointed to Tailor and Lucky.

"Good idea," Gord agreed. "You take the girls back to the ranch. If you don't mind me saying so, you all look done in."

Becky looked doubtfully from Bruce to Gord. "It *would* be a relief to get the kids back to the ranch." She motioned to the campers. "Come on, we're heading out."

She paused as the girls gathered up their horses' reins. "How will you find Jesse and Alison?" she asked Bruce.

"We'll go back to where we found the horses and track them from there," Bruce said.

"I've also been dropping chocolate bar wrappers, in case we got lost," Rachel confessed.

"Nice try," Cam laughed. "Just like Hansel and Gretel."

"All right." Becky smiled thankfully at Gord and Bruce. "You rescue Alison and Jesse and we'll go straight back to the ranch. Can you just tell me one thing first? Why didn't you two tell us you were scientists when we met you back at Burnt Creek?"

Bruce shrugged. "Scientists can be a secretive lot. I guess we don't like to talk about what we're doing in case someone tries to copy our research and publish it first."

"Or interfere," Gord added. "Like that Native guy who was tailing us—"

"That was our friend, Thomas," Becky explained. "He wasn't tailing you, he was following wild horses."

"Oh!" Gord looked surprised. "You mean Thomas Horne? We've heard about his work with the wildies. He's doing good things."

"Yes," Becky said, "he is." She and the campers shook hands with Gord and Bruce, then mounted up.

"This is more like it," Courtney sang out.

"You're right—my feet were falling off." Dee-Dee sighed. "Now we get to *ride*."

"Thanks for everything." Becky smiled at Bruce. "I hope you get lots of DNA from bears."

She climbed gratefully into Shadow's saddle, reached down and patted the little paint's shaggy neck. "I've almost forgiven you for running out on me back there," she told Shadow, "but never do that again!"

Motioning the campers to ride ahead of her, Becky shouted, "Last stretch. We'll be home before dinner."

Back at the mud slide, Alison tried to make Jesse more comfortable. He was stretched on the ground, his leg so swollen it resembled a sausage stuffed into a blue jean casing.

"It looks like it's going to burst!" Alison exclaimed as she helped him lift his leg onto a moss-covered stump. "Shouldn't we slit your pant leg?"

Jesse tried to chuckle, but it came out more like a groan. "No way! These are my favorite old jeans." He reached forward and patted his swollen knee.

"If it would help your leg, let's cut the jeans!"

"It wouldn't help." Jesse reached for her hand. "Just the opposite. My pant leg is keeping the swelling down, believe it or not. Basic first aid."

"You know a lot about injuries." Alison frowned. "Do you get hurt a lot, doing rodeo?"

"Yep. Separated shoulder, bruised liver and broken rib. And that was just last year," Jesse said with a shrug.

"Two years ago, I tore this same hamstring bronc ridin' and had to have surgery. This time it'll probably just heal up on its own."

"You're kidding."

"Nope." Jesse gave Alison a sideways grin. "Has to heal fast, too. I've got the national championship to defend in November."

Alison gulped. "Jesse, why do you do this stuff if you get hurt all the time? I thought you were studying equine management at college."

"I'm ridin' broncs and ropin' steers to win money to buy a ranch and some good horses." Jesse tried to sit up. "You can't manage equines if you haven't got 'em, or a place to keep 'em."

"Oh." Alison stared at him. "I get it. There's big money in rodeo."

"If you win," Jesse said. He lay back, grimacing with pain. "You can see why I'm not good boyfriend material, Al. At least not for the next four or five years. My life's tied up with rodeo. I'm on the road twelve months of the year." He looked at her with eyes full of hurt that had nothing to do with a torn hamstring. "Remember Julie, that helicopter pilot I was dating?"

"Sure."

"Well, she dumped me because of rodeo. Can you blame her?"

"I guess ... not." Maybe Jesse was too old for her. He was willing to spend four or five years getting torn muscles and broken bones to buy his dream ranch. It seemed so far from her own life! She was just sixteen, still thinking about having fun and going to college. And even though she'd been injured barrel racing, it wasn't part of the sport the way it was in bronc riding. There, you were *guaranteed* to get hurt!

"I'll build up the fire and get some water," Alison gulped. "Rachel left us some tea."

She started up, but Jesse grabbed her shirt and pulled her back down to him.

Alison's heart leaped. Had he changed his mind? Was he going to kiss her?

"Hold on." Jesse's whisper was harsh. "Look there—isn't that the two guys we saw at Burnt Creek Camp?" He pointed through the trees.

Alison turned and looked where he was pointing. "Yes! And they've got our horses. What do you think is going on?"

Jesse struggled to sit. "I don't know, but let me do the talkin'."

CHAPTER 23

Wreck!

Meg forgot about Jordan, her jade trophy and the rest of the group somewhere on Mustang Mountain. The foal mattered now—more than anything.

It seemed an endless ride. They'd been traveling for hours, picking their way down the narrow, winding wild horse trail. How did Thomas even know which path to follow? Meg thought. There were so many side trails wandering off into mossy valleys or up high ridges.

Finally the trail met a wider path through the trees, where the black muck was chewed up by the hooves of many horses.

"From here it's only about half an hour to the ranch," Thomas called back to Meg and Jordan as they turned onto the wide trail. "Almost home."

Meg rode up beside him. The foal hung as limp as a sack of grain over Palouse's withers. She could tell by the grim lines beside Thomas's mouth that he wasn't sure he would live till they got to the ranch. "It's going to be close, isn't it?" she asked in a low voice so that Jordan, riding behind, wouldn't hear.

Thomas nodded. "I don't want to ride fast and bounce the poor little guy around. But maybe you and Jordan could go ahead."

"Good idea," Meg said. "Jordan," she called over her shoulder, "we're almost at the ranch. Why don't you and I ride ahead and get a bottle ready for the foal?"

"Can we lope?" Jordan cried, excited.

"Sure … go for it," Thomas told her.

"All right! Let's go, Cody!" At Jordan's word, the big bay horse forged past Thomas and Meg.

Meg shot an anguished look at Thomas and urged Rocco forward. She wanted with all her heart to stay with him and the foal, but she should keep up to Jordan. They didn't need more trouble on the last leg of the trail.

It was a bad sign, she thought, that none of them had suggested a name for the young horse.

Becky and the four campers were just ahead. They had made excellent time on the clear-cut.

As they rode down the trail to the ranch, it was hard to hold the horses back. They knew food, water and a good rest waited just ahead. They bunched close, each horse wanting to be first back to the ranch gate.

When they got to the steep hill where Jordan had struggled with Rocco, all four of the campers' horses flew down it.

"Wheeee!" shouted Cam. "What a blast!"

Instinctively, Becky shouted to them to slow down, but they were having too much fun to listen. All she could do was watch.

And then Rachel, riding in front, tried to jump short-legged Shane over a dead tree at the bottom of the hill.

Becky saw Shane stumble. The other horses, riding too close, had no chance.

The wreck seemed to happen in slow motion.

First Rachel's horse went down.

Then one after the other, three other horses crashed into him. The girls flew through the air like rag dolls tossed by an angry child.

Becky pulled Shadow to a halt. There was a terrible moment of silence before the wails began.

✸

Meg and Jordan heard wild whinnies and cries of pain as they rode toward the steep hill.

"That sounds like Rachel!" Jordan pulled Cody up short.

"And Dee-Dee!" Meg stared at her. "Let's go."

They loped their horses to the top of the hill and stared in horror at the scene below. Becky was crouched beside Courtney. She lay stretched on the ground in a patch of trampled mud and moss. Rachel was bent over Cam but there was no sign of Dee-Dee or the horses.

"Becky!" Meg shouted. "What happened?"

"We had a wreck!" Rachel started stumbling up the hill toward them, clutching one arm. "Everybody's hurt except me," she cried to Meg and Jordan. "I just have a sore shoulder." She was shivering with shock, her brown eyes staring.

Meg barreled down the hill, past Rachel. She raced to where Becky was bending over Courtney and threw herself off Rocco. Courtney's face was streaked with blood. Her broken glasses dangled off one ear.

"Her glasses must have cut her eye," Becky gulped. "We shouldn't move her or take off her helmet."

"I'm okay, I'm okay," Courtney was trying to insist.

"Can you check the other girls for me?" Becky asked. "I'm so glad you're here—" Her voice broke. She took a deep breath and looked up. "Where's Thomas? Is he ...? Was he ...?"

"He's all right. He'll be here soon, but—" Meg stopped. It would take too long to explain about the wild horse foal. "Where's Jesse? And Alison?"

"They stayed behind when we lost our horses ... Jesse's hurt."

Meg and Becky stared at each other—it was just the two of them, on their own. "Tell me later," Meg said quickly. "Let me check on the girls. C'mon, Jordan."

Cam was lying flat on her back with her blonde hair fanned out below her helmet and her eyes round and wide. "My back hurts," she whimpered.

"Don't move!" Meg barked. "Jordan, stay with her while I find Dee-Dee."

Jordan nodded, clutching Cam's hand.

"What can I do?" Rachel tugged on Meg's sleeve as she ran past.

"See if you can find the horses," Meg panted. "Chances are, they've taken off for the ranch, but you never know." Rachel hurried away.

"I'm over here," Meg heard Dee-Dee's squeaky cry. She ran to where the small girl was huddled under a pine tree. "I think I've broken my wrist. It kills!" Dee-Dee was holding her right arm close to her chest. Her pointed face was as white as a piece of paper.

"Can you move your fingers?" Meg asked.

Dee-Dee carefully wriggled them. "Yes."

"It's just a bad sprain—you'll be okay," Meg promised. "Sit still and take deep breaths."

She ran back to Becky.

"Cam's the one to worry about—she's hurt her back. Dee-Dee's sprained her wrist. What about Courtney's eye?"

"I keep telling her I'm fine!" Courtney struggled to sit up. "I can see."

"There's a lot of blood, but I think it's just a cut on her cheek and another cut over her eyebrow." Becky looked up at Meg. "Go get my mom. Tell her we need medical help. I'll go look at Cam."

Meg could see the dread in her friend's face. "Don't think the worst." She steadied Becky's shoulder. "I'll ride ahead. Jordan can stay with you."

Jordan didn't argue. "I'll stay with Courtney," she offered, taking Courtney's hand.

Meg had a second to think how much things had changed since Jordan hadn't wanted to sleep anywhere near Courtney. Was it only the night before last? She threw herself on Rocco. "All right," she told him, "you've been wanting to run for two days. This is your chance."

She let Rocco out on the wide trail to the ranch. He didn't need any urging. Within minutes they burst out of the woods. The creek and sloping meadow and ranch gate were right in front of them. They'd been so close to the end of the ride! Meg hated to be the one to tell Becky's parents about the wreck.

It turned out she didn't have to tell anyone. Laurie Sandersen came running across the yard as Meg rode in.

"The girls' horses just galloped in with their reins dangling. What happened?" She grasped Meg's arm, as if for support.

"They had a crash—not far from here," Meg told her. "They were almost home. All the kids are hurt—can't tell how bad."

"At least Jesse's with them," Laurie said breathlessly. "He's got a lot of experience."

Meg gulped. "Uh—Jesse's not—Becky said he's hurt, too. He and Alison are up on the mountain near the mud slide."

Laurie clapped her hand to her chest. "So it's just Becky with the campers?" She didn't wait for an answer, just turned and raced for her horse, hurling orders over her shoulder.

"Get Claire, Meg. She's a park warden—expert at first aid and rescue. Tell her to grab the medical kit in the office and meet me in the barn. Then tell Dan to get the clinic on the radio, in case we need a helicopter. Ring the dinner bell—that'll get everybody running. And hurry!"

Meg raced to obey Laurie's orders. She dashed to the porch, grabbed the bell rope and rang the bell as hard as she could. Its wild clanging filled the air. Within minutes she'd spread word of the wreck and people were hurrying in all directions. Another few minutes and the rescue party was on its way out the gate.

Meg wanted to go with them, but Laurie had said no. "We'll manage. Stay here so you can tell Dan and the clinic about the girls' injuries," she insisted. "They'll need details."

It was only as Meg watched their horses splash through the creek that she realized she hadn't had a chance to ask Laurie about a baby bottle and formula for the foal. Thomas could be here any minute. Who else would know? Meg asked herself. She dashed into the kitchen. "Slim! You've got to help me! What do you know about bottle-feeding foals?"

Meanwhile Thomas had come across the wreck. He slid from Palouse's back, careful not to disturb the foal.

Becky was bending over Cam, talking to her, smoothing her hair.

"Thomas!" she exclaimed, glancing up. "I'm so glad to see *you*." Her voice came in short bursts. "Meg went ahead for help. Can you look after Dee-Dee and Courtney until someone comes? I have to keep Cam still. She's hurt her back."

"Of course," he murmured. He hurried over to Courtney and Dee-Dee, who were sitting propped against a pine tree. Courtney was pressing a blood-stained bandanna to her eyebrow.

Thomas gently removed the makeshift bandage. "Can you see?"

"Sure. My glasses broke when I hit a tree, so everything's fuzzy, but I'm not blind."

"She *gushed* blood," Dee-Dee squealed. She pointed to Palouse and the limp body of the foal on his withers. "Where did you get a baby horse? Is it alive?"

"He's a wild horse foal," Thomas explained quietly. "His mother was killed by wolves. He needs food. When help comes, we'll get him back to the ranch and try to feed him—hope he's not too weak to eat."

"Oooh!" Dee-Dee breathed a long sigh. "Poor little guy. I hope help comes soon, for all our sakes."

"Me too." Thomas stood up, looking for Jordan. She came running out of the trees with Rachel. "We can't find our horses," she lamented. "They took off."

"That would be their instinct so close to home." Thomas led Jordan back to Palouse and the foal. "Pat the little fellow and tell him it won't be long till he gets a good meal," he told her.

Jordan's voice quavered. "He … won't understand what I say."

"No, but hearing a friend and feeling your hand will help him," Thomas promised.

Much later, in the ranch barn, Thomas shook his head. "I was worried this little guy would be too weak to suck on a bottle, but I was wrong, wasn't I?"

The wild foal was guzzling down the special formula as fast as he could. He emptied the bottle and nudged Meg's arm for more.

Jordan watched, draped over the stall's low wall. "I thought of a name," she said. "I think we should call him J.T., for jade trophy. What do you think?"

If we have a name for him, it means we believe he's going to live, Meg thought. "I think J.T. is perfect," she told Jordan. "Have you shown the others your flake of jade?"

"No." Jordan wrinkled her brow. "They probably won't even care. They're too banged up to think about a trophy right now."

"At least they didn't have to get flown out by helicopter," Thomas said. "Claire says Dee-Dee's wrist is just sprained, and Cam has a bruised tailbone, but no injuries to her spine." He and Meg shared a smile of relief. It could have been so much worse. All of the campers' horses seemed to have escaped injury, too."

"Jesse's all right, as well," said Meg. "He and Alison got back safely, thanks to those two scientists, and Alison says his leg is already feeling better with some ice."

At that moment the ranch house bell rang. It wasn't the wild ringing of alarm that Meg had set off earlier, but a brief DING, DANG, DONG.

Meg stood and stretched. "Come on. We all need food, just like J.T."

"I want to stay with him," Jordan begged. "He's never been alone, and he'll be scared."

Meg looked at Thomas.

"We'll put him in the stall beside Shadow," Thomas said. "They're both mustangs. They'll keep each other company." He picked up the gangly foal in his arms and carried him to his new home. Shadow put her head over the stall divider and blew softly to welcome the baby. He tottered over and touched noses with her.

"See," Thomas said, "they'll be fine. C'mon, I'm starving."

"I still want to stay," Jordan said stubbornly. "Can't you just bring me back some bread and butter?"

Meg chuckled. "I know what's wrong. You think you're in for a typical Mustang Mountain Ranch Camp meal. But Ruby's cooking is a lot different than Slim's, believe me. She makes apple pies that you'll dream about."

"She's right." Thomas grinned. "You don't want to miss Ruby's pie." He and Meg had shared Ruby's pies at Sunrise Lodge the summer before.

"Okay," Jordan gave in. "But I want to come back here after dinner. I want J.T. to be my horse. He already likes me."

Thomas frowned. "J.T. is not going to stay a cute little colt you can cuddle," he warned Jordan. "In a few months, he'll be a rambunctious young stallion that won't do a thing you want him to. If you get a horse someday, it shouldn't be one who'll bite and kick and toss you off his back."

"Oh," said Jordan, disappointment clouding her face. She lifted her slender shoulders. "But I love him. What will happen to him?"

"He might come home with me, to my grandfather's ranch," Thomas explained. "I have some horses there that used to be wild."

"Or he might stay here," Meg went on, "and you could see him next summer, if you come back to camp."

If there *is* a camp at Mustang Mountain next year, she thought as they walked out of the barn. That was the big question right now.

CHAPTER 24

JADE TROPHY

As she walked into the dining room with Jordan, Meg could see that everyone was staring at Cabin 3's table.

No wonder! Laurie and Claire had declared all four girls well enough to come to the dining room, but they were still a shocking sight. Cam was perched gingerly on a pillow. Dee-Dee had her arm in a sling. Rachel was nursing a very sore shoulder, and Courtney looked frightening, even though her face had been cleaned up. Her glasses were mended in the middle with duct tape and the gash on her cheek was bandaged. She held an ice pack to her swollen eyebrow.

Meg had never seen her four campers so quiet.

As Jordan and Meg approached, the four girls solemnly laid their hands on top of their heads. Jordan sprinted ahead, dived into a vacant chair and clapped her hand to her head.

That left Meg, gaping. "What ...?" she started.

"Got you *again*!" Dee-Dee burst into giggles and the others joined in.

"Caught you, Meg!" Cam held herself tight so the laughing wouldn't jiggle her bruised tailbone.

"You're the gopher, again!" Courtney sang out.

The whole dining room erupted into cheers and laughter.

"I guess I can quit worrying about you guys!" said Meg. "Believe me, it will be my pleasure to serve you poor starving invalids."

She sailed off to the kitchen and soon staggered back with huge bowls of spaghetti and meatballs, fresh salad and homemade garlic bread on a tray.

"You're in for a treat," Meg sighed as she sat down. "The best spaghetti you've ever tasted."

Dee-Dee whined once about how hard it was to eat with one hand, and Cam squirmed uncomfortably on her pillow, but for the next twenty minutes, no one said much as they gobbled up the food. Meg went back for a second bowl of Ruby's spaghetti and they slurped that down, too.

Finally, there was apple pie—as delicious as Meg remembered it.

She gazed around the wood-paneled room. Everyone seemed to be enjoying Ruby's amazing pie. Twelve hours ago, Meg thought, we wondered if we'd ever make it back. Now, here we all are, warm, full and having dinner like a normal riding camp.

When everyone was finished, Laurie stood on the fireplace hearth to make an announcement.

"Before campfire tonight, I want you to make a special effort to tidy your cabins. Tomorrow is visitors' day. We'd like to make a good impression on anyone who pays us a visit."

Cam said quietly, "I think my parents are flying in by helicopter tomorrow. At least, they said they would."

Meg swallowed hard. Cam's parents—the heritage minister and his wife—coming tomorrow? Could the timing be any worse?

"Also!" Laurie shouted above the conversation in the room, "tonight the campers from Cabin 3 are back, but they've had a very challenging out-trip. We'll understand if they're too tired to make it to the campfire."

"I guess we won't go," Rachel sighed. "We never got our jade trophy."

"And now the stone horse is gone forever," Cam added.

"I'm too tired anyway." Courtney pressed the ice to her eyebrow. "All I want to do is sleep."

"Will we have to clean up our cabin tonight?" Dee-Dee flapped her sling. "I can't do much with this—"

Jordan spoke up. "I—I think we should go to the campfire," she said. "I have a surprise. If you come to our bunkhouse now, I'll show you."

They all gathered around Jordan's bunk. Cam lowered herself carefully onto the pillow at the end of the bed. Slowly, Jordan pulled back the blankets. The green stone glowed against her white sheet.

For once, the other campers were speechless. They stared at the stone.

Finally, Dee-Dee choked, "Wh-where did you get that?"

"From the cave in the stone horse's nose."

"You mean it was just sitting in there like a big green booger?" Courtney gasped.

"Don't be so crude!" Cam laughed. She reached out and touched the stone. "Is it really jade?"

"Thomas says it is." Jordan nodded eagerly. "He tested it with his hammer. When he hit it, it made little white lines, like a feather."

"Wow!" gasped Rachel. "Our jade trophy. It's amazing. And no one will ever be able to get another one like it."

Meg stood behind the admiring group. "This piece of jade wasn't just sitting in the cave. Why don't you ask Jordan how she got it?"

"How did you …?" Rachel blurted.

"I went up to the cave last night," Jordan began.

"By yourself?" Dee-Dee squeaked.

"Well … Thomas was already out trying to save the wild horses because the wolves were all around us, and Meg was asleep."

"The wolves!" said Courtney. "We heard them, too."

The other girls listened with their mouths open.

"Meg wouldn't have let me go if I asked, so I just went," Jordan explained.

"Awesome!" Courtney's battered face cracked into a grin.

"How far did you have to go?" Rachel gasped.

"I'm not sure. It was up this steep hill Rocco had already dragged me down. Anyway," Jordan went on, "when I got there, I found this huge green boulder, but it was too heavy to move. I couldn't even budge it."

As she went on, telling how Thomas had split the trophy from the big boulder, the four girls crowded closer around Jordan. They picked up the jade, admiring its color, holding it to the light. Rachel put her arm around Jordan's shoulders. "I take back every mean thing I ever said to you," she apologized. "You're not a wimp, you're a hero."

"You did it for us," Cam gulped. "For Cabin 3."

"You were exceptionally brave." Dee-Dee shook her head solemnly.

"Tell us about the foal you brought back, and the wolves," Courtney begged.

"I'll tell the whole story at the campfire tonight," Jordan promised.

As dusk deepened on Mustang Mountain, Thomas and Chuck lit the large fire they'd built in the firepit on one side of the house. Here, the hill fell away, making natural seats for an audience. Long log benches were set around a flat sandy circle in front of the fire, forming a stage.

Meg had painted the stone horse on a bed sheet to hang behind the fire. Lit by the flames, the black horse on the white sheet seemed to dance.

"That looks terrific." Thomas held Meg's hand as they studied the effect.

"I hear you've been helping Chuck with another surprise." Meg squeezed his hand. "Can you give me a hint?"

"Just one." Thomas smiled down at her. "It involves two mystery visitors."

"Thomas! Who's here? Tell me!" Meg pleaded.

Chuck strode over to them. "That would spoil the surprise. In fact, don't tell Alison or Becky even that much. We want to amaze them!"

It was growing dark outside the circle of firelight. Flashlight beams bobbed down the path to the fire-pit. Sparks leaped in the air. Up above, the stars were coming out. As the campers took their places around the stage, Meg saw her small group hobble and limp to their places in front.

Alison came rushing up. "Chuck, I heard you're master of ceremonies. What have you got cooked up for tonight's campfire?"

"You'll see." Chuck raised one eyebrow at Alison. "Where's your cowboy?" he grunted gloomily.

"He's not *my* cowboy and he's staying in his room to rest his hamstring." Alison sighed.

"Too bad." Chuck shook his head. "Come on, Thomas, we should get ready for the show." Thomas let go of Meg's hand with a final squeeze. "See you later."

"He's so romantic," Alison sighed again. "Too bad Jesse's missing all the fun. He won't even come and just sit around the fire."

"Can you blame him?" asked Meg.

"I guess not." Alison shrugged impatiently. "It was a rough ride back, even though Bruce and Gord helped as much as they could."

Becky joined them. "Hi, guys," she said. "I guess this is Cabin 3's big night. Is Jordan here? I saw her at the ranch house a few minutes ago, trying out her trophy on the mantle."

"She's down in front." Meg pointed. "This is one time she's not going to be late."

"I'm happy for her," muttered Becky, "but I can't help wishing it was Cam who brought back the prize. It was her idea in the first place, and her parents are flying in tomorrow. They're going to find their daughter barely able to walk. Not much of an advertisement for Mustang Mountain Ranch Camp." She looked around the glowing scene and sighed. "This might be our last campfire."

All three of them were quiet, thinking about what tomorrow might bring.

Suddenly there was a burst of music from a guitar and drums.

CHAPTER 25

CAMPFIRE

Chuck marched onto the stage. Thomas shone a bright, battery-powered searchlight on him.

"Welcome to our nightly campfire," Chuck announced. "We have some very exciting news from Cabin 3, who have just returned from their out-trip. But first ..." He paused dramatically.

Another searchlight lit up the left side of the stage.

"... I want to introduce you to my new horse."

Alison sucked in her breath. "New horse?" Chuck had lost his horse, Copper, last summer in a wilderness accident. Had he finally found a replacement?

"And here she is," Chuck went on. "Campers, meet Sally."

Into the circle of light pranced two people in a horse costume. The head of the horse had a long blonde mane.

Her body was a camp blanket. Four feet in riding boots stuck out below.

"Sally is a very special horse," Chuck announced. "She can talk. Say something, Sally."

Sally performed a low bow. "Hel-lo," she said in a low throaty voice. "I'd like to ask Chuck a riddle. Why did the cowboy throw his horse over the fence?"

Chuck took off his hat and scratched his red head. "I don't know. Why?"

Sally did a little dance. "Because he wanted to see a *horsefly*. Get it? Horse. Fly?"

Chuck groaned. "Can't you do better than that?"

"Okay. Why did the pony go to the doctor?"

"I'm afraid to ask."

"Because he was a little *hoarse!*" By now all the campers were howling with laughter at the fake horse.

"Who's in the costume?" Meg whispered to Becky.

"I don't know … maybe my parents?"

The horse was still clowning around the stage, followed by the searchlight. "One more," it said. "Why did the mare scold her foal? … Because it was *horsing* around!"

"Those are the worst jokes I've ever heard! You've embarrassed me in front of all these people!" Chuck cried. He chased Sally around the stage, grabbing for her tail. He caught it and pulled. The costume slid off and two laughing people jumped up to take bows.

"It's Rob! and his sister, Sara!" Becky leaped to her feet.

Chuck was introducing them. "Ladies and gentle-men, the front end of my horse is Sara Kelly. She's come to help teach riding at the camp. The hind end you al-ready know—Sara's brother, Rob, counselor for Cabin 3, now recovered from a bad bout of flu and back, we hope, to stay."

There were cheers and whistles from the audience.

Becky ran on stage, flinging her arms around Rob. "I'm so glad to see you. You're really better?"

Rob hugged her back. They left the stage to more whistles, with Rob whispering in her ear, "I'm much better, but Sara would only let me come if she came, too. She wants to keep an eye on me."

"It doesn't matter." Becky clung to him. "You're here, that's the important thing."

In the audience, Alison nudged Meg. "You remember Rob's sister Sara from the Stampede? The kids are going to love having lessons with her—she's one of the best barrel racers in the west."

"And now," Chuck announced as the stage cleared, "it's time to hear about the out-trip. The kids in Cabin 3 have chosen their youngest member, Jordan, to tell the story. Jordan, can you come up here?"

Jordan walked shyly into the light, carrying a large basket. She didn't show anyone what was inside until the end of her story. By then, the fire had burned low and everyone was on the edge of their seats. Thomas im-itated wolf howls to accompany her tale of climbing up to the cave to find the rock. Then, with a flourish, Jordan pulled the jade out of her bag and held it high. "Our trophy!" she announced.

There was a hush, then wild applause and more whistles. "I'd just like to thank my cabinmates, Rachel, Courtney, Cam and Dee-Dee, for the trick they played on Meg," Jordan added over the applause. "If they hadn't sent her up the wrong trail, we never would have got separated and I would never have got up to the stone horse." She turned the jade rock so the light gleamed on it.

In the audience, Courtney, Dee-Dee and Rachel looked sheepishly over at Meg. "Sorry!" Courtney whispered.

There was another outburst of cheering.

Chuck came back to his announcer's role. "Cabin 3's trophy sets a high standard for all out-trips in the future. And now, it's late, time for Taps and our beds."

The campers and counselors formed a ring around the fire, singing into the darkness, "Day is done ..."

"I hope there is a future," Becky said to Meg as the chattering and laughing campers headed up the hill to their bunkhouses in a parade of flashlights. "Now that Rob and Sara are here, we have a better chance of making the camp a success. I'm just afraid it's too late— when Cam's parents see her—" She shook her head in the darkness. "If only I had been able to slow the girls down on that last hill."

"Just be glad all the kids are okay." Meg squeezed her arm. "We were *so* lucky nobody was badly hurt! You go and celebrate Rob's getting back, I'm going to check on J.T."

Meg headed for the barn.

As she hoped, Thomas was already there. Meg slipped in beside him. "How's our baby doing?"

"He's been frisking around playing, eating—you can almost see him grow," Thomas answered softly. "He's finally fallen asleep for a minute." The foal was curled up with his nose on his tail.

"This is the first time we've been alone," Meg said in a low voice. "I haven't had a chance to say how much I hope—" she gulped, but she had to say it, "hope you'll stick around."

"I'll be here as long as you are, Meg."

Meg felt dizzy with relief. "Oh. I thought you might leave as soon as you could to trail that wild horse band."

Thomas put his arm around her. "I'll get Chuck to help me round up the band later, once the camp's closed. Maybe we can all ride with them up to my grandfather's ranch."

He hugged Meg closer. "We're lucky, you and I. It's not very often people find the person they want to be with for the rest of their lives as young as we did. I miss you every minute we're not together."

"Me too," Meg whispered. She was dying to throw herself at Thomas, but that was the wrong thing to do. Thomas didn't want to rush things—her best chance of keeping him near was to just let him keep talking.

"I watched you with Jordan and this foal," Thomas went on. "I know what's in your heart. I know I'll love you all my life."

He bent and kissed her.

Meg couldn't say anything for a long minute. Then she told Thomas her plans. "I'm fast-tracking through school," she said in a rush. "By next fall, if I get in, I'll move out here to go to college. And—" she laughed breathlessly, "I'm even trying to get my mom and brother talked into moving west. Mom could have a good business in Calgary."

"A year," Thomas murmured. He dropped his arm from around her and straightened up. "That's not too long. In a year, J.T. will be a strong young yearling. He's going to be a beauty."

"It *is* long!" Meg protested. How could Thomas talk about a horse at a time like this?

He put his arm around her again. "I know," he said. "But it will pass before you know it. And it helps to think of other things."

Meg laughed shakily. "Okay, but don't get so busy with your horses that you forget to write or email."

"This year—" Thomas kissed her again, "I promise to do better."

***

Back at the firepit, Alison was trying to convince Chuck to let her help put out the fire.

"Let me ..." she offered as he went for another pail of water.

"I told you already, I can do this myself," Chuck

growled. "Go look after your friend—that rodeo cowboy of yours."

"Chuck! I said I was sorry. It's just that Jesse and I go back a long way, and I was surprised to see him and—"

"And a rodeo champ is a lot more exciting than a regular rancher, that's it, isn't it?" Chuck set down the pail and glared at Alison in the dying firelight.

"I thought you did a great job of running the campfire," Alison said lamely. She hadn't realized Chuck was this mad. "You looked like a natural up there."

"Don't try to put me off!" Chuck glared at her. "I'd like to know where we stand."

"Oh, Chuck ..." Alison heaved a long sigh. "I'm not ready to get serious with anybody. I realized that on this trip. Jesse's too old for me," she went on. "He's grown up, if you know what I mean. And I'm not. Please, Chuck, can't we just go out and have fun, without all this 'forever' stuff?"

"I guess so. Thanks for giving it to me straight." Chuck handed Alison the bucket. "Put out the fire. Then let's go up to the office and see if there's a party going on."

The next afternoon at one o'clock, Heritage Minister Henri Perrault and his wife, Lise, stepped out of the helicopter and made their way toward the waiting campers of Cabin 3 and the camp staff.

"Wait till they see what's happened to their pre-cious daughter," Becky groaned. "It's too bad, because the girls have come a long way, especially Cam. But all her parents will see are cuts and bruises and slings."

Sure enough, shock spread over Henri Perrault's handsome face as he caught sight of Cam, perched on her pillow on a folding chair. "What happened to you?" he gasped.

Becky waited for the words that would mean the end of the camp.

"Dad! It was awesome!" Cam's face lit up. "Rachel started the whole thing ..."

Dee-Dee flapped her sling up and down in excitement. "We were flying down this hill—"

"Yeah, we were going really fast—" Courtney interrupted.

"Because we were STARVING!" Rachel shot in. "So I jumped Shane over a log, but he didn't make it, so—"

"Let me!" Courtney shoved her duct-taped glasses higher on her nose. "Let me tell it! Rachel's horse didn't make the jump. He stumbled, and then *my* horse, Flint, ran into him, and I flew off and broke my glasses, and then—"

"I ran into Courtney," Dee-Dee shouted, "and my horse just took off like a rocket and we were speeding through the trees and I tried to hang on, but I couldn't and I hit the ground and sprained my wrist!"

"You should have seen it, Dad," Cam giggled. "It was a total wreck." She wriggled on her pillow. "Spencer tried to stop, but he ran into Courtney's horse, too, and I slid off his behind and landed on mine."

Then they were all laughing and talking at once, while Cam's stunned parents looked from one happy, excited face to another.

"Were any of the horses injured?" Lise Perrault inquired.

Laurie Sandersen stepped up to answer. "No. We were very lucky. And none of the girls are seriously hurt."

"They seem to have had a wonderful time." Cam's mother shook her head. "I've never seen my daughter so, so, *animated*. Her hair's messed up, and she's *laughing*!"

"It was great, Dad!" Cam was telling her father. "We were in two avalanches, and in the last one, this enormous stone horse fell off the mountain almost on top of us!" She paused. "—and best of all, look at this!"

Cam held up the flake of green jade that she'd been hiding under the edge of her pillow. "It's our out-trip trophy, Dad. It's pure jade. Jordan found it on top of the mountain."

Henri Perrault reached for the rock. He held it in his hands and turned it in amazement. "So, the legend was true." He smiled around at the campers, the counselors, Dan and Laurie Sandersen. "This will help me in my fight to save Mustang Mountain Ranch as a place of cultural importance. So many people urge me to turn it over to private hands—"

"But you wouldn't do that, would you?" Cam begged.

"So, you *like* this Mustang Mountain camp?" Cam's mother looked confused.

"Of course I like it. We're all coming back next year, and the next year, and as long as we can, aren't we?" Cam turned to the other campers.

There were eager nods of agreement all around.

"Then I suppose we will have to make sure the camp continues to operate," the heritage minister said. "I'm proud of you all," he told the whole group, but his smile was for Cam.

"Thanks, Dad." She beamed back at him.

Becky, Meg and Alison hugged one another.

"Race you to the house," Becky sang out. "This deserves a celebration."

In the kitchen, she opened bottles of fizzy mineral water. "Nearest thing we have to champagne." The three of them took their drinks out to the front porch in the sunlight.

Meg looked around at the ring of mountains surrounding the ranch. "I'm so glad Mustang Mountain Ranch is going to survive. It's such a big part of my life, I can't imagine it not being here."

"A big part of all our lives," Alison murmured. "Think of everything that's happened to us since we rode up here in that snowstorm, two thirteen-year-old city kids."

"And one ranch kid who'd just moved here and thought she hated the place," laughed Becky. "You two changed that."

"We've all changed." Alison sighed.

"But we'll always be friends." Meg smiled at the two cousins—so different, and so much alike. She lifted her bottle. "Here's to our future."

"To our future!" Becky and Alison echoed as the three of them clinked their bottles together.

Sky Horse #1

Meg would do almost anything to get to Mustang Mountain Ranch, high in the Rocky Mountains. She wants a horse so badly. A sudden storm delays the trip and begins an adventure that takes Meg, her friend Alison and Alison's cousin Becky far off the beaten track. To reach Mustang Mountain, they'll need every scrap of courage they possess.

ISBN 1-55285-456-6

Fire Horse #2

Meg, Alison and Becky are alone at the Mustang Mountain
Ranch. When two horses go missing, the girls and their friend
Henry set out on a rescue mission. Caught in a forest fire, they
save themselves and the missing horses with the help of a wild
mustang stallion.

ISBN 1-55285-457-4

Night Horse #3

Returning to Mustang Mountain Ranch for the summer, Meg, Alison and Becky meet Windy, a beautiful mare about to give birth to her first foal. Meg learns a secret too: a bounty hunter has been hired to kill the wild horses in the area. When Windy escapes the ranch, the girls move to protect the mare and the wild horses they love.

ISBN 1-55285-363-2

Wild Horse #4

On vacation at a ranch in Wyoming, Meg, Alison and Becky have a chance to ride wild horses. Alison doesn't care to participate. Her mood threatens the vacation. She changes, however, when she discovers a sick wild horse. As hope for the sick horse fades, Alison must conquer her anger and come up with a plan to save it.

ISBN 1-55285-413-2

Rodeo Horse #5

Alison and Becky prepare to join the competitions at the Calgary Stampede. Becky wants to find out more about Rob, the mysterious brother of a champion barrel racer. Meg meanwhile is stuck in New York, longing to join the Stampede. An accident threatens the girls' plans. Or was it an accident?

ISBN 1-55285-467-1

Brave Horse #6

A phantom horse, a missing friend, a dangerous valley filled with abandoned mine shafts ... Not exactly what Meg, Alison and Becky were expecting on vacation at the Mustang Mountain Ranch. Becky had expected a peaceful time without her annoying cousin Alison. Alison had expected to be traveling in Paris. And Meg had planned to meet with Thomas. Instead, the girls must organize a rescue. Will they be in time?

ISBN 1-55285-528-7

Free Horse #7

New adventure begins while Meg and Thomas care for a neighboring lodge and its owner's rambunctious 10-year-old stepson, Tyler. The trouble starts when Tyler opens a gate and lets the ranch horses out. In his search, Thomas discovers that someone is catching and selling wild horses. Could it be Tyler's brother Brett and his friends? A hailstorm hits and Thomas fails to return to the lodge. Can Meg and Tyler find Thomas and save the wild horses?

ISBN 1-55285-608-9

Swift Horse #8

Alison Chant is angry at the world. She wants a new horse, but everything gets in her way. First, her mom says, "No more horses!" Then, she finds the horse of her dreams, but it belongs to a young girl named Kristy Jones, who refuses to sell her beloved Skipper. Finally, Alison takes matters into her own hands, only to get Skipper and herself into terrible trouble at a barrel race. Who can save her? Does she have the courage and strength to make things right?

ISBN 1-55285-659-3

AN IMPRINT OF WHITECAP BOOKS

Dark Horse #9

Becky Sanderson has entered her first endurance challenge, the Wildflower 50. She and her mother's chestnut mare, Windy, have to race 50 gruelling miles over rough, steep mountain trails. Becky is confident she can do it, especially with the help of her friend Rob. But Rob unexpectedly gets distracted by another racer, a willowy blonde whose behaviour is more than a little suspicious. Will Becky's jealousy get in the way of her finishing the race? The competition gets tougher, and for some of the riders it seems there's more at stake than first place. Becky finds herself caught up in a vicious race with riders who will stop at nothing to win.

ISBN 1-55285-720-4

ABOUT THE AUTHOR

As a child, Sharon Siamon was crazy about two things— books and horses.

Born in Saskatoon, Saskatchewan, Sharon grew up in a farming area of Ontario. She learned to ride by coaxing a farmer's big workhorses over to rail fences with apples, then climbing on their backs and riding bareback till they scraped her off under the hawthorn trees that grew along the fence. She wished for a horse of her own and read every horse book she could find.

Sharon has been writing books ever since for kids who dream of having adventures on horseback, among them *Gallop for Gold* and *A Horse for Josie Moon*. The Mustang Mountain adventures began with a wilderness horseback trip through the Rocky Mountains. Sharon's friends in the exciting fields of barrel racing and endurance riding have kept the adventure going. So far, the Mustang Mountain books have been translated into Norwegian, German, Finnish and Swedish.

Sharon writes back to all the fans who write to her at her email address: sharon@sharonsiamon.com.